I0724330

WOLF FATED

FORTITUDE WOLVES - BOOK TWO

NICOLE R. TAYLOR

Wolf Fated (Fortitude Wolves - Book Two)

Copyright © 2021 by Nicole R. Taylor

All rights reserved.

This book is written in British/AU English.

No part of this book may be reproduced in any form or by any electronic or mechanical means, including information storage and retrieval systems, without written permission from the author, except for the use of brief quotations in a book review.

www.nicolertaylorwrites.com

Edited by: Silvia Curry

CHAPTER 1
SLOANE

ourage.

The word was losing all meaning, especially in the face of all I'd been through. When death stares you in the face, you soon learn the truth in it.

In the distance, I could see the smudge of the dirty air, lights, and concrete of Melbourne. It was a warren of roads and buildings, a cesspool of glitz and glamour with mid-tones of middle-class suburbia and shadows of supernatural life.

I was finally going home. I'd grown up in Melbourne, but after my mother's death, it'd become something sinister.

Chaser moved beside me. Glancing at him, I saw the colour wasn't returning to his skin. He'd been shot in the heart with a wooden bullet, and as a vampire, it'd been a fatal blow...except he wasn't a normal vampire. He was bound by magic to the Fortitude Wolves's alpha—*my father*—and it'd been the only thing that'd saved him.

He looked sickly, his skin grey, withered, and washed out. He'd lost a lot of blood and the little he'd taken from me hadn't been enough to revive him.

His body was slumped in the passenger seat, his head lolling to the side. His iridescent eyes were bright and alert, so at least I didn't have to worry about him desiccating on the Calder Freeway.

Chaser was... Well, there was a lot to him. He was this rough, devilish, bad boy with messy hair, scratchy stubble on his jaw, and the fashion sense to boot. Leather jacket, tight T-shirts, tighter jeans, and combat boots. He had a tattoo on his chest, but I didn't even know what it was because I was always too caught up in his gaze. Chaser had this thing with direct eye contact. When he had you in his sights, you simply couldn't look anywhere else.

He had a perpetual scowl on his face, but when he turned on his heart... *Damn.* He'd taken a lot of heat in my name since he walked into my life—he'd been a literal human shield. His arrival might've started out as a direct order from my father, but we'd transformed into something else, something unexplainable.

The vampire I wanted to hate but loved instead.

The vampire who'd told me the truth about who I was.

The vampire who'd stood by me as I'd turned into a wolf for the first time.

The vampire I'd killed for.

He'd taken my innocence, but I'd given it freely. Now we were on the road to something bigger.

Revenge. Answers. *Freedom*.

The Fortitude Wolves would bow to their new alpha, and Chaser would find justice for the one he'd lost...and his freedom from the spell that bound him to the pack.

At least, that was the plan, but whether it turned out that way or not was another story entirely. There were too many variables to know how this was going to end...or how long it was going to take.

"Let me do the talking when we get to the compound," Chaser said, breaking the silence.

"Why?"

"They're not friendly wolves and they don't know you. You didn't grow up in the pack. Loyalty is a big thing to these men. There's a hierarchy bound by supernatural blood, one that's not easily broken."

"I know I have a lot of work to do," I told him. "I know they won't trust me right away."

"I'm not doubting you."

I didn't want to argue, not when I didn't understand what I was walking into and whether they would look after Chaser. There was no way I was walking into the Fortitude compound with my rage on. There was too much I didn't understand about being a werewolf *and* the supernatural world at large.

Right now, I needed to have a clear head when I finally came face-to-face with my father. He would not manipulate me, not this time.

"Listen, Sloane," Chaser said, his voice strained, "if we're doing this, then they can't know about us and they can't know you turned."

My hands tightened around the wheel. I knew we had to play this carefully. I had to hate Chaser for bringing me back, even though I wanted nothing more than to claim him in front of the entire world. Our screwed-up road trip had brought us together, and now it was over. What we'd been through was nothing compared to the war I'd just signed us up for.

I had to be prepared to make sacrifices. *Big ones.*

"I have to go back to doing what I was doing," Chaser went on. "You have to forget about me."

"I could never forget about you."

He snorted, his silent and deadly 'I don't want to talk about it' mask sliding back into place.

"I didn't know the truth," I went on, already annoyed with how this was starting to work out, "but now I do. Now I understand...at least, a little."

Chaser grunted, turning his head away from me.

"You owe justice to Loretta, but you deserve it, too," I continued, fixing my gaze on the road ahead. "We're not going to end up the same way. I won't allow it."

"Glad we're on the same page," he drawled.

"This isn't the time to be an arsehole," I snapped. "I saw the photo, you said 'wife,' and I flipped. What was I supposed to do? We were on the run, I didn't know who to trust. I was still reeling from turning—honestly, I still am—and..." I wanted to run away with him. "You didn't exactly make it easy."

"Nothing in life is easy, Sloane. Predators rule. Love is—"

"Love always wins," I interrupted, refusing to look at him. "I have to believe that."

"I wouldn't hold onto *that*."

My hands tightened on the steering wheel as I took the exit towards the northern suburb of Coburg. "We're almost there. The last thing I want to do is argue."

Chaser grunted, his hand finding my thigh. The contact made me shiver, but our dysfunctional relationship was quickly becoming the least of our worries. We would have time to figure us out. We had to. I needed to. Fortitude wouldn't be forever.

"You're still reeling from your first transformation," he said after a moment. "We still don't understand what it means."

"The full moon is gone, but I still feel different," I told him.

"How?"

"My eyesight is sharper, my sense of smell is turned all the way up... I reckon if I tried, I'd be stronger, too."

"Don't try in front of anyone."

I snorted. "Of course not."

He fell silent, his gaze moving towards the city. We'd merged off the freeway and into slower city traffic, and my heartbeat had taken on an irregular rhythm. I knew he heard it, but I'd be a fool not to be at least a little afraid.

"T-minus five minutes," I said. "Any last words of wisdom?"

"Don't break eye contact. Wolves are all about dominance."

"I don't plan on it." I flicked on the indicator and turned down a side street, leaving the traffic behind.

"You know your way around," Chaser remarked.

"Bad memories always stick."

Ahead, I could see the Fortitude compound lurking out of the half-light. It was bathed in the orange glow of the streetlights overhead, but the sign outside was lit up like a beacon.

Fortitude Customs was painted in bright blue over the double garage, and a graffiti-style mural was plastered over the entire side wall. Motorcycles, skulls, flames, and the crossed swords the pack had taken for its emblem in modern times. Beyond was a factory-styled building.

"It's bigger than I remember," I said as we approached.

"Most of the pack lives here," Chaser said. "The building out back has been converted. Bedrooms, common rooms, kitchen, storage, the works."

"And a business out the front." I grimaced. They'd set themselves up in the modern world, putting up a human front for their supernatural shenanigans.

Chaser gave my thigh one last reassuring squeeze as I turned off the road and passed a lineup of cars and motorcycles out front.

I brought our car to a stop on the oil-stained concrete outside the garage, my skin crawling when I saw several pairs of eyes turn towards us.

Big, mean, beefed-up men rose to their feet, the clang of tools echoing their deliberate steps towards their unexpected houseguests. Several reached for weapons, and I swallowed a ball of fear that had risen in the back of my throat. I'd imagined something like this, but seeing the wolves in the flesh was an epic wake-up call.

Chaser opened the door and practically fell out onto the grease-stained concrete. The man at the front of the group reached out and pulled him to his feet, not even commenting when Chaser shoved him away.

Climbing out of the car, I rested my hand on the roof and narrowed my eyes at the group of men who'd just seemed to realise I was standing there. My skin crawled as I was subjected to the ultimate staring contest.

There were six of them, all big, dirty, and cut from the same dangerous cloth. Tattoos, scruffy beards, scars, muscles, flannel shirts, leather vests, bandanas... I breathed deeply and got a nose full of wet dog, oil, and grime that almost made me gag. They must be all werewolves if they smelled like *that*.

"Chaser," the man at the front of the group said. "We were starting to think you were strung up somewhere."

"Don't worry about me," Chaser drawled. "Worry about the other guy."

"Some entrance," the wolf said before giving me the once-over. "This her?"

He nodded. "Where's Butcher?"

The man whistled, and a scrawny guy at the rear of the garage ran off, disappearing into the building. Then he nodded at the other men. "DeLuca, Rocket, get Chaser inside."

Butcher? I curled my lip, knowing it was in my best interests to keep my mouth shut.

The man's gaze fixed on me, and I stared right back. His bulk was intimidating and paired with his full beard, hard lips, and fully tattooed body, he was one mean-looking piece of work. Most people would've shied away, peed their pants a little, or made a break for it, but I wasn't most people.

No one said a single thing for a full minute. The two guys known as DeLuca and Rocket hesitated, and Chaser leaned against the car, watching me closely. Weapons were still drawn and hadn't been put away when they realised their token vampire was home with his cargo.

These were the wolves I was hoping to win over? *The mountain just got a whole lot steeper...*

"Put the guns away," Chaser said with a roll of his eyes. "I'm half-starved, but I'm not hungry enough to go for any of you."

The men holstered their weapons and turned their attention to me.

"She looks like a wallflower," one of the wolves stated. "This really her?"

"That's her all right. She put down a vampire," Chaser said, his voice loud in the silent garage. "A bullet through the heart. Didn't even blink."

"And she didn't want to put one in yours, too?" the tattooed wolf asked, still staring me down. His hostility crawled all over my skin like slime. *I'd have to watch this one.*

"Settle the hell down, Harley," Chaser snapped. "She understands what this is about."

The wolf eyed me and then stepped away from Chaser. "Get the vampire inside before he dries out. Betty—"

"Don't call me Betty," I said, my voice low and full of warning.

Chaser smirked and threw his arm around DeLuca's—or was it Rocket's?—shoulder.

"Boss'll want to see you," Harley snapped. "*Now.*"

Slamming the car door closed, I glared at the man who was at least three times the size of me as I rounded the bonnet. Ignoring the eyes trained my way, I followed Harley to the right while Chaser was hauled off to the left. I would face the next part alone, but I always knew it would be this way.

It was time to go see Daddy.

CHAPTER 2

SLOANE

The alpha of the Fortitude wolves, my father, Anthony Marini, had never been a bundle of sunshine and rainbows.

I'd always been a little frightened of him as a child. When I got into trouble, he was quick to anger, and my mother made sure I was never alone with him. She took the brunt of his foul temper for my sake, keeping me away from him and his criminal life as much as she was able to.

Now, I was in the middle of it and had learned the hard way it wasn't as it seemed.

I glared at the back of Harley's head as he led me into the compound. He looked like he had a fair whack with the ugly stick, and I wondered, besides working in the garage, how much whacking he did of his own.

It had been a long couple of weeks, and I'd forgotten when I'd last slept. My eyes burned every time I blinked, my entire body felt like it was one large bruise, and I was running on fumes, but I still followed him without complaint. Thinking about Chaser, I knew he would fare better than I would. Vampires seemed indestructible, especially when they had spells binding them into servitude.

Harley led me down a dark hallway, then into a common room. Glancing around, I was greeted with more wolves. What felt like a hundred carbon copies of Harley glanced up and stared at me, their eyes raking over my body and sizing me up. Women glared my way as the men leered, making my skin crawl.

I painted my face with a mask of nonchalance. No fear or emotion. Cold eyes. Hard mouth.

The hazy air in the room reeked of cigarette smoke. Music was playing in the background, some old rock 'n' roll record, while the clack of balls flying across the pool table caught my attention.

A hand grabbed my arm, and Harley wrenched me towards him. "Don't stare, sweetheart. Predators take it as a challenge."

"*Let me go,*" I snarled.

The room fell silent with all eyes on us. This was my debut moment in front of the people I needed to win over.

"You don't get to touch me," I said, wrenching away. "*I'm a Marini wolf.*"

"You're nothing, *little girl.*"

I curled my lip and took a step closer, challenging him. "What was that you said about predators?"

Harley snarled and pulled me forwards, dragging me through the common room and into another hallway. When we were out of sight, he pushed me against the wall and curled his big, greasy hand around my neck.

"You've got a big mouth on you, Betty," he murmured. "Around here, big mouths get people into trouble. You don't want to get off on the wrong foot. You might be Marini's daughter, but that won't save you."

I shoved down the wave of fear welling up inside me and smiled the sweetest smile I could manage. "The moon isn't full, so I guess we'll see about that...*won't we?*"

He snarled and tightened his grip. "*Bitch.*"

"You need to learn how to respect women."

"*Harley.*"

He froze, his grip loosening.

"Let her go," the voice commanded. "That's not the way to treat my daughter."

Harley's lip curled and his eyes burned with unmasked loathing. Leaning close, he delivered a threat directly into my ear. "Daddy won't always be around to save you, Betty."

Letting me go, he strode off down the hallway towards the common room, leaving me against the wall. I was hyperaware my father was standing a handful of steps away.

I didn't want to look him in the eye, but I had to. There was no avoiding it.

I turned my head slowly, my heart pounding in my chest. How one man could cause such fear was chilling. I knew what he was capable of. I knew who he was. I knew what he'd done to my mother. Now I had to cozy up to him so I could stab him in the back. It would hurt—*oh, would it hurt*—but the look on his face when he realised I'd taken everything from him would be worth the salt in the wound.

He'd aged considerably in the last fifteen years, but it was his eyes I noticed first. His Italian heritage shone through in their chestnut colouring, but they couldn't be any colder. His short, scrappy beard was strewn with grey, and his severe, short back and sides haircut gave his hard angular face a menacing look. Broad shoulders, a hard chest, and a towering stature completed the picture. A picture was worth a thousand words and all of them said '*don't trust me.*'

Anthony Marini was a big man. Bigger than Chaser. Bigger than that vampire Bailey. But not as big as Harley.

"You've got your mother's looks," he said, picking up a strand of my hair and rubbing it between his forefinger and thumb. The baritone of his voice was gravelly, as though he'd smoked a thousand cigarettes a day until his throat had turned raw.

"You're acting like you never saw me before," I snapped, pulling away.

"You've changed."

"It's been fifteen years. I grew up," I said, implying I would fight with deadly force if I had to. "*A whole lot.*"

He nodded towards the door behind him. It was a silent command—the alpha asserting his dominance. If I was supposed to feel anything supernatural, I wasn't sure, but I needed answers...so I obeyed.

Dad—I wasn't even sure I should call him that—held out his hand, gesturing for me to step into the room like he was some kind of reformed gentleman. I wasn't on the road with Chaser anymore. If he was the one standing there, I would give him lip, but he wasn't.

Where was he?

The room beyond was large, part of a suite made up of a private sitting room with posh leather couches, a sleek bar fridge, and a massive, flat-screen television. A private bathroom and bedroom completed the presidential suite, all fitted out with the latest mod-cons. Marini was alpha, so he took what he was owed.

My gaze flickered around the room and settled on the automatic rifle mounted on the wall, and the handgun and long-barrelled revolver on the glass-top coffee table. The grip on the revolver was inlaid with mother-of-pearl.

Dad closed the door behind him and crossed the room. Sitting in the armchair, he leaned forwards and rested his elbows on his knees, waiting for me to take a seat.

I lingered behind the couch, my eyes on the guns in front of him. Did the air have a tang of copper to it, or was it my imagination? I could smell tobacco, spice, gunpowder, and something else...the same stench I'd caught a whiff of outside. Did werewolves all smell like wet dog?

Taking in the room, I was aware of him watching me as I saw the patched hole in the wall behind my head. I promptly stepped to the side.

Dad raised his eyebrows and resigned himself to the fact that I wasn't sitting anytime soon.

"Did he hurt you?" he asked, his voice familiar yet oddly strange to my ears.

"Who?"

"Chaser. Did he take care of you?"

"Yes." I narrowed my eyes, not liking what he was implying.

"Did he touch you?"

"No."

Dad watched me closely, taking stock of my answer. Chaser had fed from me only hours before, but Dad couldn't know that. He would cut Chaser open top to tail if he knew, and I'd be right back on the pack's list of items to sell—if I wasn't on it already. The vampires seemed to want me for a blood surface, after all.

"He was shot," I went on. "He desiccated and—"

"Butcher will patch him up," Marini interrupted.

"He did his job. He should be rewarded."

He grunted, his lip curling. "Will you sit down?"

Tensing, I rounded the back of the couch and perched on the edge. My thighs burned, and my back thanked me for it, but it was a bed I longed for the most. A bed, sleep, and knowing Chaser was going to be all right. Maybe I should've been thinking about my own fate, but I was running on fumes.

"You will be given a room in the compound," Marini stated. "You're free to come and go as you please, but you are not to leave under any circumstances."

"That's the direct opposite meaning of 'free to come and go as I please,'" I pointed out.

"If you need something, ask. Don't bother Chaser with your inane requests. I know he saved your life, but that does not make him your errand boy. We have new recruits who specialise in those things. Ask them for your tampons."

I snorted and rolled my eyes.

"So, when does the bidding start?" I drawled.

He stared at me and didn't bother replying. His fingers stroked his beard while his eyes retained their icy lustre.

"The vampires attacking you is a slight on me," he began, lowering his chin. The light bounced off his face in a demonic way, making my spine tingle. "It makes me look weak. You know I'm not weak, Betty.

They've declared war on Fortitude by putting a hit out on you."

I snorted. He really thought I'd buy that? Fortitude was going to war over me? The more likely scenario was that he wanted to sell me to the Hollow Men for their blood ritual.

"Betty died," I said, lowering my voice to match his tone. "Fifteen years ago."

"Ah, you call yourself Sloane now." He smiled. He actually smiled at me like I was a cute little child playing grown-up games. "So, tell me, *Sloane*, how much of our world did you know about before Chaser retrieved you?"

I tensed, my lips thinning. "None of it."

"And what do you know now?"

Werewolves, vampires, witches... *A wolf who could turn at will, who was not enslaved by the curse binding her kind to the moon.*

"I know you're a werewolf," I said. "An alpha. All those people out there...they're wolves, too. Chaser is a vampire, and there's a bunch more that are after me. Then there are other wolves, from other packs, who would like to see me dead, too." I narrowed my eyes and wrapped my arms around my stomach. "I wouldn't know why. I'm ordinary. I've never..."

Marini smirked. "Turned on a full moon?"

"*No.*"

He laughed and shook his head. "How *fortunate* for you."

"Why?" I asked. "Why me?"

"Because I'm the alpha of the Fortitude Wolves, the dominant werewolf pack in the entire state...and you're my only daughter."

It was a lie, but I said nothing.

I swallowed my anger. "Then why aren't I like you?"

"Your mother was human, Sloane," he told me. "You take after her."

One statement was a lie, and the other I wasn't sure about. Was my mum human? The thought hadn't crossed my mind, and I regretted not slowing down and asking Chaser about her. He hadn't met her, but maybe he knew anyway.

"So, I just have to stay here?" I demanded. "Just because I'm your daughter? A daughter who you haven't seen in fifteen years, by the way."

"Yes," Marini drawled. "Where you stay and how you are treated depends on your attitude."

"You could've had something good," I murmured. "It could've been great, you know, but you screwed it all up." I reached out and picked up the revolver, knowing full well it wasn't loaded. I stroked the mother-of-pearl, watching the colours shimmer. "I'm half her, but I'm also half you."

"Is that what you want?" The undertone of his smile changed, and the leather creaked as he leaned back in the armchair. "To be acknowledged?"

Setting down the revolver, I rose to my feet, trying

not to vomit on the way up. "It wouldn't even matter. *I'm human*. It's not like I can be alpha, is it?"

He nodded, the ice in his eyes beginning to thaw. His gaze never left mine as he took a mobile phone out of his pocket and brought it to life.

"You must be tired." He pressed the screen. Lifting the phone to his ear, he added, "Rick. My daughter is here. Get in here and show her to her room. Get her whatever she wants," he looked at me, "*within reason*."

He put the phone away, and I wrinkled my nose as the door opened.

A man strode into the room, dressed in beat-up jeans, boots, and a faded Harley Davidson T-shirt. He had a shaved head, stubbled jaw, and soft eyes to match his baby face. A new recruit. I made a mental note to ask him for tampons.

"Rick, this is my daughter *Sloane*."

I stepped around the couch, glad to get away from the dangerous tug of war that'd begun with my father.

The newbie wolf nodded, eager to serve his master like the desperate dog that he was. "Room's this way."

I took two steps before I stopped.

"Dad?" I turned, leaving Rick out in the hallway.

My father lifted his head and waited for my pearl of wisdom.

"If you ever try to hurt me again, the last thing you'll see is my face as I put a bullet in your head."

"Of course." He smirked, lips curving lopsidedly. "You *are* half me."

CHAPTER 3
CHASER

DeLuca and Rocket dragged me through the garage, through the compound, and into Butcher's room.

Sloane was gone, I was back in my revolving-door nightmare, and the game had already begun.

"Did you get a look at her?" DeLuca declared.

"That's Marini's daughter?" Rocket asked before letting out a slow whistle.

I shoved down my jealousy—another human emotion I hadn't felt for almost a century—and sat heavily, my arse hitting the chair with a dull thud.

Sloane and I had been on the road together for almost two weeks, and it was safe to say I'd gotten used to having her all to myself. Now she was gone and the sensation her absence gave me was strange and unfamiliar.

"What happened out there?" DeLuca asked as I rested my elbow on the table.

"Shut your pie holes," a booming voice declared behind me. "He ain't gunna tell you dogs nothin'."

Butcher appeared in my peripheral vision, but I smelled him long before. Like a lot of the guys around here, he was built like a tank. The wolves called him the grey giant, but the name he'd earned from the alpha of the pack was much more accurate.

Before he'd joined the Fortitude Wolves, Butcher had been a paramedic, but his reckless behaviour had gotten him banned, and his underlying werewolf tendencies led him to a life of patching up the wolves he now called his brothers. Overseeing my emergency blood bank was just an added bonus.

I wouldn't go as far to say I liked him, but at least I knew where his loyalties lied.

"What was it this time?" Butcher asked. "Bullet, stake...?"

I'd had just about every kind of injury I could think of...and died of a couple, too.

"Wooden bullet," I replied, still aware that DeLuca and Rocket hadn't left the room. I pressed the heel of my hand against my heart.

"She do it?" Butcher gave me a look, his silvery eyes full of suspicion.

I shook my head. "One of *them*."

Butcher glared at the two wolves and jabbed his finger at the door. "Quit your starin'. Bugger off."

Rocket snorted and strode out of the room with DeLuca on his heels. I got that some of these guys wanted to be on the in, but there was a hierarchy for a reason.

Butcher opened the stainless-steel industrial fridge and took out a hospital grade blood bag. I hated that I had to go to him for blood—yet another form of control the pack had over me.

"If it wasn't for that spell of yours, you'd be dead by now," the big man mused. "How long have you been all wrinkled like that?"

"Ten hours."

Butcher grunted, knowing a lesser vampire would've snapped and gone on a feeding frenzy by now, and slapped the blood bag into my hand. "Get that in ya before you shrivel up entirely."

Tearing open the top, I drank greedily, the blood soothing my burning hunger. Feeding from Sloane had tided me over, but it wasn't nearly enough.

Once I finished the bag, Butcher gave me another.

Staring across the room as he waited for me to finish, my thoughts zeroed in on Sloane. She would be standing before her father right now, saying God knows what.

Was he going to lock her up? Was he going to sell her to the Hollow Men? Was he going to tell her the truth?

The only thing I knew for sure was that I was sick and tired of suffering for the pack's greed.

"You're starting to fill out, boy," Butcher said as I sucked the last of the blood out of the bag.

"I'm older than you," I remarked, tossing the bag. "Watch yourself."

"You're a hack, Chaser," the wolf drawled. "A real butcher."

"Look who's talking."

"What happened out there?"

I gave him a pointed look. He could ask all he wanted, but I never talked about what I did. *Never*. The bond didn't forbid it, but it was best to keep my mouth shut.

The door opened, interrupting our intimate moment, and Rick appeared. He was newly welcomed into the pack, eighteen and with only a few years of full moons under his belt—a pup playing a wolves' game.

"Marini wants to see you when you're done," he said, glancing at the blood bags on the table.

Narrowing my eyes, I wiped the back of my hand across my mouth. Looked like I was going to find out what happened to Sloane sooner rather than later. It'd been a long time since I'd had someone to worry about—not since Loretta—and I wasn't sure I knew how to deal with it.

The little wolf scowled. "*Now*."

"Careful," I said, my lip curling. "You may be Marini's new chew toy, but it doesn't mean you get to order me around."

"You better listen to what the vampire says, *boy*." Butcher nodded. "The alpha may have singled you out, but it's not because of your intelligence." Rick opened his mouth, but the wolf barked, "And don't you even think of talking back."

I stood, my gaze fixed on Rick. He was desperate to impress...which made him stupid and dangerous.

"Don't rip the kid's head off," Butcher said, glaring at Rick but talking to me. "I know two bags wasn't enough."

I smirked as Rick paled and edged past him a little closer than necessary. Hearing the change in his heartbeat, I chuckled and left the wolves behind.

I made my way through the building, dodging eye contact with anyone I passed—not that they wanted to talk to me. I was the token vampire, the slave who did the alpha's bidding. No one wanted to mess with me.

I didn't see hide or hair of Sloane, but I knew I wouldn't. I didn't know when I would see her again.

Marini was sitting in his armchair when I dragged myself into his rooms. He loved that damn chair. Why, I didn't know, but his arse was permanently grafted to the thing.

"Another memento added to the collection," he said as I closed the door behind me.

I grunted and walked over to the couch, masking the spark of humanity behind my eyes. My scars— even though they physically healed—were a painful reminder of the servitude I'd been tricked into. So was the tattoo on my thumb and the psychopath sitting in front of me. They weren't a memento for my scrapbook.

"My daughter says you should be rewarded," Marini went on. "Anything I should know?"

I gritted my teeth to keep from saying something I'd regret.

"You dropped the ball on this one, Chaser. Big time." He picked up the revolver sitting on the coffee table and flicked open the chamber. Taking out some wooden bullets from his shirt pocket, he loaded them one by one in slow, deliberate moves. "Bodies left behind, shots fired in *public*."

"They've upped their game," I said, anger bristling up my spine. "We were forced to take an alternate route. I don't know how they tracked us, but they were connected enough to block out an entire train with no prior planning. They ambushed us."

Marini stared at me, his expression passive. He was a hard man to read at the best of times, but right now, he was blank. When he was like this, he was capable of his absolute worst.

"What are you going to do with her?" I asked.

"Be careful what you say next," he snapped, closing the barrel on the revolver. "While you're bound to me, you can't die, but I can make it *hurt*."

"I went to great lengths to get her here. I want to know if it was worth it." The words burned my throat as they came out. Sloane *was* worth it. Took me time to realise it, but she was. I cared about her. When a killer cared about someone, things were destined to become messy.

Marini snarled and waved the gun at me. "In the two seconds she's been here, she's made an enemy out of Harley, threatened me, and showed a weakness for *you*."

"I can see the parallels," I drawled. "Difficult was an understatement when I went to get her."

"Shut the hell up with your clever words," he snapped. "What did you tell my daughter, Chaser?"

"I told her what she needed to know," I replied. "I couldn't hide what I was if she was to remain alive."

"Did you tell her what she is?"

"*Did you?*"

Marini's expression dropped and the room went silent. We were the only two supernaturals in it, but it was like the air turned cold and someone pressed the mute button. He was holding a gun and had a reputation for using it—as recently as the day before I left to get Sloane. I noticed the plaster had been repaired at least.

"She's back in her old room for now," he said after a moment. "What happens next depends on her attitude...and yours."

"I delivered her," I said. "My involvement in her fate has ceased."

"Just like that, eh?" He was baiting me, waiting for me to take a bite out of him.

"Unless you order me to." I gritted my teeth. "You know that."

"Yes." The alpha smirked and put the revolver down. "I do."

"What are you going to do about the Hollow Men?" I asked, fishing for my own answers. "They won't stop now that she's here. You may have bought the pack a reprieve, but it's only a matter of time."

Marini wasn't having it, though. "You're damaged goods, Chaser. You don't get to ask me questions. *Get out of my sight.*"

Leaving the alpha and his bloodthirsty tendencies behind, I went to my room—a tiny hole with a bed, a window, and not much else. When I opened the door, I saw my bag sitting just inside. Closing myself in the room I'd called my prison cell for the past seven years—the last time the building was renovated—a wave of exhaustion finally smacked me in the face.

All the humanity I'd been holding back since the train came flooding in, the emotions making my ears ring and my temples throb. My body had returned to normal, but my mind was another thing entirely.

I collapsed, my vision slipping before my head even hit the pillow, and my last thought was of Sloane.

CHAPTER 4
SLOANE

Waking up without Chaser glaring at me was an odd experience. It didn't feel right.

Light was pouring through the slats in the venetian blinds, casting long fingers over the end of my bed. I rolled over and rubbed my eyes, groaning when my entire body throbbed.

Last night had been a strange experience.

Rick had delivered me to my old room last night. Strangely, everything was just as I'd left it the night I'd run away, almost like Dad believed I would come back someday. A double bed sat against the far wall, a desk with a stereo in the opposite corner, a black shag-pile rug was spread out on the floor, and someone had put my bag in the closet. My dirty clothes were missing, and I hoped it meant someone was washing them.

Fancy that, a wolf pack who did laundry.

As for my father, *Marini*, I didn't believe a single word he said. I wasn't safe here.

Keep your eye on the prize, Sloane.

Dragging myself out of bed, I opened my bag and found the last of my clean underwear and a change of clothes. I set them on the desk, leaving my broken laptop beside them. University had become a distant memory, and my textbook had probably disintegrated at the bottom of that lake by now.

What did I even want to be, anyway? There wasn't a course on taking over werewolf packs, was there?

My hair was greasy and I smelled funky. I needed to scrub myself until I was raw to get Bailey's stench off my skin. The world would *not* miss the dead vampire.

I shuffled into the bathroom and closed the door behind me. Turning on the light, I stripped out of the travel-stained clothes I'd slept in, and my thoughts went to Chaser when I saw the blood on my jeans.

Where was he? I knew he could more than look after himself, but he wasn't invincible. He'd been so grey, his skin shrivelled...

I glanced at my reflection in the mirror and hesitated. Lifting my hand, I ran my fingertips across my cheekbones. Looking down at my naked body, I remembered the sensation of my bones breaking as I'd stood underneath the stars on the Nullarbor.

Despite the agony, I wanted to turn again. The realisation startled me, and I closed my hand around the edge of the basin...which cracked under the pressure.

Gasping, I jerked away. I still had the strength of the full moon behind me. I had to be careful.

What a mess...

It hadn't felt like it, but I'd been tossed about so much in the past two weeks it was a miracle I'd reached the other side. I was finally realising just to what extent now that I had a moment to slow down and be alone with my thoughts.

I'd turned into a wolf, shot at, flung from a car, beaten up, killed a vampire, betrayed by Chaser's past...and survived everything that'd happened on the train to the point of finally admitting that I'd fallen for him.

A vampire.

And he had, too. He hadn't called it love, but he'd admitted his feelings. He wanted to run away with me. He wanted to disappear with me and forget everything...but he was bound to Marini by magic. He couldn't leave.

Chaser was a slave and I was hunted. I'd never be safe out there on my own.

Turning on the shower, I ducked under the hot water and scrubbed my skin raw. Emptying the little bottles of body wash and shampoo I'd taken from one of the many motels we'd stayed at, I eventually stepped out a lot cleaner than I had felt in days.

A woman was sitting on the end of my bed when I

emerged from the bathroom. I yelped, suddenly glad I'd dressed in there and not wandered out in the buff.

"Hey, I'm Sam," she said, her voice not much louder than a hushed whisper.

She reminded me of Yvette in a way. She was tiny, blonde, and pretty...even with the bruise on the side of her face.

"You're Sloane," she added when I didn't acknowledge her.

I nodded, noting the fact she hadn't called me Betty. *Good.* Taking out a comb from my bag, I brushed out the tangles in my wet locks.

"What happened to your face?" I asked, leaning against the desk.

She lowered her gaze and shrugged. "I fell."

I snorted. *I bet.*

Sam's blue eyes widened. I intimidated her, that much was clear. I wondered what stories had been going around about me. I was pretty sure it wasn't anything good, which meant I had a lot of work to do.

"How old are you?" I asked, looking her over. She was so delicate, it was hard to tell.

"Twenty-four," she replied. "My mum always said I had a baby face. I always get asked for ID when I go to the bottle shop, so I just hand it to them with the cash. Saves them from asking the question. It gets tiring."

I tilted my head to the side and dragged the comb through my hair. Seemed like little Sam was starved for attention if a little flower like her couldn't answer a simple question without telling me her life story. Whoever her man was, he wasn't treating her right. Not by a long shot.

"I'm a year older than you," I said, my heart bleeding a few drops for her. "I suppose that's why they ordered you to follow me."

"Follow you?"

Marini didn't believe me, I realised. He knew I hadn't told him the entire truth, so he'd sent in the most vulnerable woman in the entire place in an attempt to soften me. Sam was just the poor, unsuspecting pawn in the middle of a deadly play for power. It wasn't her fault, and I'd help her if I could, but not at the expense of losing my freedom...or what little of it I had.

"I know how these things work. Don't worry about it."

"Harley said—"

"Harley?" I scoffed and shook my head, tossing the comb onto the desk. "That explains a lot."

"He said you needed someone to help you out," Sam muttered. "You were here alone and needed someone to talk to."

I sighed. "All I want to know is where's the food? I'm not permitted to leave, so you know." I waved my hand at my stomach, which growled on cue.

"I can help you with that," Sam declared, her eyes brightening. "I like to cook."

Shrugging, I followed her from my room and through the compound.

It was quiet today. Everyone seemed to be somewhere else, but the smell lingered.

"So," I asked as I followed Sam, "are you a...*you know*."

She glanced over her shoulder. "A werewolf?"

"Yeah."

"No, I'm not, but I carry the gene."

I hesitated. "The...gene?"

"That's how it works. My mother was a wolf, by my father wasn't. It was a fifty-fifty chance, but when puberty came and nothing happened, I soon found out." She paused and I almost smacked into her. "Are you?"

"No," I lied. "I guess I got the other fifty, too."

Sam shrugged and kept walking. "It's probably a good thing. I hear turning hurts like hell...not that I've seen it."

The kitchen turned out to be huge. A large table that could easily seat twenty ran the length of the room, while the walls were lined with cupboards, two refrigerators, an industrial-sized oven and range, a giant double sink, and two microwaves. I was rather surprised to see a posh Nespresso coffee maker on the bench. I didn't think werewolves were refined enough to want a macchiato with their French toast.

"What do you like?" Sam asked. "Pancakes?"

"Pancakes?" I frowned. The best I'd hoped for was cereal.

"Sure. Leave it to me."

I sat at the table as she busied herself with making the batter from scratch—no premix packets or anything. It was all eggs, flour, and milk. It was rather...*homely* and threw me off balance.

It seemed Sam's forte was looking after people like a mother hen. She was small, human, and lacked confidence, but give her a lost soul to care for and she was all in. She was the kind of woman destined to be a sweet kindergarten teacher who wore floral dresses and baked cookies. Fortitude was the last place I'd expected to find someone like her and I wondered what her story was.

"Hey, what's this? Sam's cooking," a booming voice declared.

"Pay dirt!" someone else added.

Boots thumped on the floor behind me, and I glanced over my shoulder as three men filed into the kitchen. From the way they smelled, I knew they *were* wolves.

First in line was one of the more handsome men I'd seen in this place. Tall, muscled, tattooed up to the eyeballs, complete with a hipster beard and warm eyes. The second wasn't as alluring as he was scrappy, bald, and had beady little eyes. The third was built, tattooed, and had a lopsided curve to his mouth.

"Just in time," Sam said. "Have a seat."

"Pancakes!" the tattooed man exclaimed. "*Best*."

The wolves busied themselves getting out syrup, jam, and butter, then tossed cutlery and plates onto the table. Sam beamed and dished up pancakes straight from the frying pan and onto everyone's plates.

The tattooed man with the beard sat across from me and piled butter and syrup on his stack. "You're new."

"Yeah," I replied as a pancake appeared on my plate.

"I'm Ratchet," he said, glancing at me. "That's Rocket," he pointed to the bald guy, then to the other tattooed wolf, "and Spike."

I recognised Rocket from last night. He'd carried Chaser into the compound with some other guy. I wanted to ask about him, but I bit my lip.

"I've seen her before," Rocket drawled, sitting as far away from me as he could. "She's Marini's daughter."

"That could mean one of two things," I said, reaching for the butter.

"Which are?" Spike asked.

Sam shrank back into the corner, focusing on washing out the frying pan. She mightn't have the animal instincts, but she could sense a fight for dominance a mile off.

"Either I'm a murderous little bitch or I'm the best you've ever had." I smirked and smeared my pancakes with a healthy dob of yellowish butter.

Ratchet laughed and thumped his fist on the

table. The motion dissolved the tension in the air, and everyone's shoulders slouched. The sound of cutlery scraping against plates filled the room once more.

Liking me wasn't enough. In order for my plan to work, they had to respect me. Men like these didn't drop everything for a pretty face. They were wolves and would only bow down to absolute power.

Rocket narrowed his eyes at me before going back to his pancakes. He wasn't so convinced.

Ignoring him, I stuck a fork into my pancakes, deciding that Sam was one hell of a cook.

"Don't worry about him," Ratchet said, glancing at Rocket. "He's always got his hackles up about something."

"So you're Marini's daughter, hey?" Spike asked. "The one Chaser went to get?"

"Like there's another," Rocket muttered.

Spike snorted. "That we know of."

"Yeah, that's me." I nodded, my heart leaping at the mention of Chaser. "The *vampire* came and *got me*."

Rocket raised an eyebrow but didn't say anything.

"Do you have any tattoos, Sloane?" Ratchet asked.

Knowing I told none of them my name, I curled my lip. "No."

"I have a shop a few blocks from here," he went on, "but I do stuff at the compound, too. I've tattooed almost everyone here."

My thumb ached. I got his meaning loud and clear.

If I wanted to be a part of the pack and play the game, then I had to *be a part of the pack.*

"Oh, I'm not a werewolf," I told them. "I don't think it'd fly."

"She doesn't have the balls," Spike said.

"Do you guys like watermelon?" I asked.

"The hell?" Rocket declared.

"When you shoot a dumb wolf in the head, his skull explodes like a watermelon. The skin splits down the sides, bone shards crack, and brains fly everywhere. Wet, sticky, and messy *as.* It's not at all like shooting a vampire—they just shrivel up like a mouldy little raisin."

Spike choked on his pancake. "*She's mental.*"

"If you guys don't stop trying to do your creepy werewolf dominance thing on me, that's what I'll do to your head," I snarled, then gestured to myself. "This is a domination-free zone."

Spike snorted and waved his knife in the air. "Marini all over."

"Pencil me in," I said to Ratchet. "I'm game."

"Tonight," he replied. "Since we've been ordered not to let you leave."

"That's a surprise." I rolled my eyes.

"See you later...*Sloane.*"

Ratchet pushed his chair back and stood, the others following suit. They left the room, leaving their dirty dishes behind. Immediately, Sam rushed forwards to clear up.

"You shouldn't make them angry," she whispered. "Ratchet's nice, but the others..."

"Don't worry about me," I said, knowing I had the strength of the full moon behind me always. "I can take care of myself."

"You're really going to let them tattoo you?" She seemed scandalised. "They don't tattoo non-wolves."

I shrugged. "I don't intend to get taken advantage of ever again."

"You mean..."

"Don't look so shocked, Sam. You heard Spike." Standing, I helped her clear the rest of the table. "I'm a Marini, and Marini's don't get sold, they do the selling...wolf or no wolf."

CHAPTER 5
SLOANE

The common room was full of women when Sam and I finally left the kitchen.

Looking them over, I wondered if it was the weekly book club meeting, but no one who ever read Tolstoy dressed in cropped *Metallica* T-shirts, denim cutoffs, and platform heels.

Suddenly, I was the odd one out, though I'd always skewed a little to the side of any group I was in. I was the tomboy with my combat boots and sour disposition. I would rather sit with the guys and hash it out, but around here, the segregation between the sexes was as black and white as ever.

Sam wandered into the centre of the fray without a care in the world. These were her people much more than the men were. With the men, she'd rushed around trying to please them, but with the other women, she was just...present.

"Sloane, c'mon," Sam said, waving me over.

The group stopped their chatter and looked up at the mention of my name. Five pairs of eyes zeroed in on me in various shades of curiosity, and not all of them were friendly.

"That's Kelly, Shondra, Emily, Raquel, and Sierra," Sam went on, introducing them all. Blonde hair, chestnut, blonde, red, and black. "This is Sloane."

Some of them smiled, but mostly, they pouted and glared, giving me the once-over—probably determining my threat level.

Oh shit, how do I relate to other women? Oh, that was right, I didn't know how. What did they talk about? Makeup, boys, who they had it in for this week... Uh, that was probably me.

Sitting beside Sam, I returned the appraising glares, making my judgments and storing it for later. First impressions weren't always an accurate indicator of someone's personality. Their actions, rather than their words, would betray them in the end.

Their smell, however...they all reeked of werewolf, but I wasn't sure if that was because of their association with the pack or not. Sam smelled the same, even though she was human, and I was sure I still carried Chaser's sickly vampire scent from our time on the road.

"You know how to make an entrance," Raquel said, blatantly looking me over. I was sans-makeup, wearing a pair of jeans, a stonewashed T-shirt with a panther printed on the front, and my trusty pair of steel-capped combat boots.

"The last time I saw a woman stand up to Harley, it didn't end well," Shondra declared. She smiled sweetly at Sam. "No offence, Sammy."

I swallowed my tongue. Some friends they were. I had to keep reminding myself that this place and these people weren't good...not yet. They thrived on the power of fear and violence. Even the women were embroiled in their own psychological warfare, all scrambling for a place at the top of the pack. Somehow, I had to get to the pinnacle and stay there.

"I don't let a man define my worth," I said, staring Shondra down. "I'm the only person who has that right. Same for you."

"Feminist crap," Emily scoffed. "The only worth around here is keeping the wolves happy."

My lips thinned. "So, are you all...?"

"Wolves?" Kelly asked. "Yes. We all turn, if that's what you mean."

"As if we don't have enough monthly problems to deal with without the full moon," Sierra said, rolling her eyes.

"I'm sorry," I said.

The women stared at me—half of them looked like they wanted to throw down, while the other half seemed bewildered.

"That you have to go through that," I added. "Turning every month must be painful."

The air seemed to clear a little, and Shondra shrugged. "You get used to it after a while."

As I sat there, I began to wonder if my blood could be used to *help* the werewolves, rather than serve as a blood sacrifice for the vampires. Maybe there was a way to use it to free the entire pack from the curse of the moon...but only if they followed me.

"So..." I smiled and looked around at the women. "Supernaturals, huh?"

Kelly's mouth fell open and she elbowed Emily. "*She didn't know.*"

"How could you *not*?" Raquel quipped. "You're Marini's daughter!"

"Well, for starters," I began, "I've *never* turned into a wolf..."

Movement in the doorway pulled my attention, and the words died in my throat. My gaze met Chaser's and my heart leapt. I wanted to run to him and throw myself into his arms, but I sat still.

He was standing in the common room watching us talk among ourselves. How long had he been there? Long enough to hear me lie about turning, that was for sure.

"Chaser," I said, nodding. Bland, indifferent, frosty. Hopefully convincing.

He narrowed his eyes and turned his back, crossing the room. The colour had returned to his skin; the greyish desiccation that had made him look so sickly was gone. When he disappeared, the maw that'd opened in his absence split open again. We'd been apart for less than a day, and I was already floundering without him.

"You really spent all that time alone with him?" Kelly asked, flicking her blonde tresses. "The *vampire?*"

"Gossip in this place is out of control," I muttered, my gaze still on the door Chaser had disappeared through.

"There's a lot about you," Emily declared. "Care to let us know what's true?"

"I'm not sure I could help you," I told her. "I seem to be in the dark as much as anyone."

"Why did you go with Chaser, then?" Kelly asked. "Start there."

"I went with him because it was that or wind up dead in a gutter someplace," I shot back.

"What do you mean?"

"The vampires are out to get Fortitude," I said, the half-truth rolling off my tongue so smoothly, it surprised even me. "I don't have a lot of love for Marini —that gossip is true—and we have a lot to work out, but I'm not into sitting back while innocent people get killed. Especially when I can do something about it." The women looked at one another, trying to decide what to do. "I don't know why I'm important. I'm just a human. Maybe it's just because I'm the alpha's daughter. If this is going to be my lot in life, then I'm going to make the most of it. Protect it. Make it a home."

They didn't look entirely convinced, but I knew it would take time. I had to play their game.

"I trust the men," Emily declared. "Wolves know how to protect what's theirs. Pack rules."

"I'm sure they do," I replied. *But so do I.*

"Did you really kill a vampire?" Sam asked, her voice barely a decibel above a whisper. "At breakfast, you said…"

All eyes were on me.

"There were two of them," I began slowly. "Chaser got one, but the other… I shot him in the heart."

"He owes you," Kelly murmured like it was a special privilege.

"Kel, if he owed you, you'd use it to make him sleep with you," Raquel said, rolling her eyes.

"*Duh,*" the blonde drawled.

"What about Stewie?"

She batted her eyelashes. "What about him?"

"We don't owe each other anything," I said, curling my lip. "As far as I'm concerned, we're even."

"*Your loss.*"

"So, what do you do around here?" I asked, changing the subject now that things had started to thaw between us. Too much Chaser talk had made me uneasy…and a little jealous. "For fun and stuff?"

"Drink, go shopping, get our nails done." Kelly looked me up and down. "But you don't like those things, am I right?"

"I wouldn't mind a set of claws, but unfortunately,

Marini has asked me to stay in the compound for the time being." I held up my hand and inspected my fingernails. "I've never had them done before. It could be cool."

"What colour?" Sierra asked.

I smirked. "Black."

"Was there any doubt?" Shondra snorted.

"I definitely have a style," I retorted.

"Tough rock chic," Emily quipped. "I like it. It's dangerous."

"She fits right in, then," Raquel declared.

"I can do your nails for you," Sierra went on. "I used to be a nail technician before the pack took me in. I have a kit, so I can do them right here."

"She doesn't do nails for just anyone," Sam whispered in my ear. "Just so you know."

"Cool," I said to Sierra. "I'm game."

"I can do all kinds of patterns. I've got some diamantés."

"Not the bloody diamantés," Shondra exclaimed.

"Shut up," Sierra shot back. "They're cool."

"Let's just start me off with plain black," I said. "Where do you want me?"

Sierra stood and held out her hand, wiggling her fingers to show off her handiwork. "Girl, come with me. I'll hook you up."

By the time the sun went down and the compound hummed with the sound of men returning, I was sporting a new set of fake nails, black and sharp, and had developed a tentative friendship with the female wolves. It was a start, but when Ratchet walked into the common room, his gaze found mine instantly.

He was looking for me.

I hadn't forgotten his offer and my subsequent acceptance, but now that he was here, the gravity of what I was about to do hit me. I was about to get marked by the pack. Something no 'human' had ever done. Marini was going to flip.

I rose to my feet, aware of the eyes watching me. Apart from the women I'd hung with that day, no one else had approached me. To many, I was still an unknown quantity, and I would remain that way until I proved myself. Words meant nothing if I didn't have the courage to back them up.

I followed Ratchet from the common room, through the compound, and to his rooms. To my surprise, Sam came with me, not wanting to leave me alone with the big bad wolf. It seemed she took her duty of keeping an eye on me *very* seriously.

Ratchet's room was cleaner than I had expected to be. He had a little tattoo station set up in one corner. There was a set of drawers where he kept all his inks and tattoo guns, a seat with a wide armrest, an old office chair, and a floor lamp that bent in all kinds of directions.

"What'll it be?" Ratchet asked. "A butterfly?"

I laughed and shook my head. "Do I look like a butterfly to you?"

Ratchet smirked and sat in the office chair, eyeing Sam. "You sure you want to be here?"

She swallowed hard.

"You want one, too? A little flower or somethin'?"

"I, ah... Harley will be looking for me," she muttered before scurrying out the door.

Ratchet frowned but didn't comment on her behaviour. He'd deliberately scared her off. How Harley treated her must be a well-known fact around here. *And they let it happen...* But something told me Ratchet was in a preventative mood, and knowing that made me look at him from a slightly different angle.

"Marini know you're doing this?" he asked.

I sat in the chair. "Of course not."

He shook his head, then began setting up for the tattoo. He pulled on some latex gloves and sprayed down the armrest with a bottle of disinfectant, wrapping it in plastic wrap when he was done. He got out a tattoo gun from one drawer and hooked it up, sliding a fresh needle into the barrel.

I sat in the chair and set my hand on the plastic wrap as he turned on the lamp, angling it over us.

"What, no flash book to flip through?" I asked.

Ratchet shook his head. "I've got a little something I prepared earlier."

I eyed the wolf and sighed. "This morning wasn't a happy accident, was it? He told you to tattoo me."

"This marks you as part of the pack," he warned. "I don't know what he's got going on with the vampires, but he wants to make sure they know who you belong to."

"I don't belong to anyone," I snapped.

"You might not be a werewolf, Sloane, but you are the daughter of the alpha. It's not just the vampires who need to understand that. It's rival packs, too."

I gritted my teeth as he placed the preprepared stencil and pressed it down. Inspecting the crossed swords, I felt like throwing up, knowing I'd been played. *I was the one supposed to be doing the playing, but here I am, getting the same brand as Chaser...* I might not be subject to the spell that bound him, but it was a brand marking me as property all the same.

"Just do it," I snarled, leaning back.

Ratchet snorted, but he didn't stop what he was doing. He filled a little red cap full of black ink and smeared some clear ointment on my finger. Reaching for the tattoo gun, he hooked it up to the power supply and pressed his boot on the pedal. The room filled with a buzzing sound as he adjusted the speed the needles were flying at.

The needle moved across my skin and the vibration shot through the bone. As soon as it started, Ratchet lifted the gun and wiped at the line, removing the excess ink from my thumb. Then he went again, following the purple lines of the stencil until he'd completed the whole design. He cleaned it off one last time, then moved away.

"There," he said, rolling the chair back and dipping the tip of the gun into a cup of water. The machine buzzed as he cleaned the ink from the barrel.

Lifting my hand, I wiggled my thumb. It was a little red and angry, but it felt all right.

"Not so bad," I said, delivering my verdict.

He laughed and shook his head. "You want it to heal properly, so put some of this on it." He tossed me a little tube of cream. "It doesn't matter how it looks, it just matters that it's there. Don't pick at the scab."

"It scabs? *Gross*." I made a face and hoped no one noticed when my supernatural blood healed it before it was due.

"Welcome to the pack, Sloane," he said. "*Strength in adversity*."

CHAPTER 6
CHASER

I leaned against the wall and blew out a sharp breath.

My returning humanity was overloading my senses, making my head spin, and the sight of Sloane had long forgotten feelings assaulting me from every angle. It'd only been a day since she'd had driven into the garage, and we'd been separated. *A single day.*

I downed another mouthful of liquor from the bottle in my hand, the alcohol soothing the burn in my throat, and continued down the hall.

Sloane's room was down here.

Leaning around the corner, I saw the hallway was empty. No one was watching, but I knew it was a test. Marini was waiting to see what she would do before deciding her fate. The Hollow Men had thrown a spanner into the works, but the only person he believed had the right to harm her was him.

The game would end before I allowed that to happen. If Sloane was going to lose, then I would be there to get her out, despite the brand keeping me tied to the pack. No hesitation.

Her door was locked. Taking out the key I'd lifted from Rick, I slipped it into the lock and turned. When the mechanism clicked, I twisted the knob and slipped into the room beyond.

The lamp beside the bed was on, casting a warm glow on the plain white walls, and I leaned back against the door as Sloane's gaze met mine. My heart twisted, reminding me of the first time I'd seen Loretta. I'd loved her before I lost her, and now Sloane...

"What are you doing here?" she asked, rising to her feet. "You can't—"

"No one's watching," I replied, turning the lock on the door. "I wouldn't be here if they were."

"Chaser, there are security cameras in the hall."

"There *was*."

She bit her bottom lip and my gaze dropped. I'd spent so much time fighting my returning humanity, and now I had to pretend I didn't care. I'd never had a lot of patience, and this was a high-stakes game I did not want to be playing right now. Sloane's pull was too strong, and all she was doing was standing there.

I closed my eyes, and the world went dark. Across the room, I heard her sharp exhale.

"There's an endgame to all this," she murmured.

"What were you doing today?" I asked, opening my

eyes. The sight of her knocked me sideways for the second time.

"Making friends."

"Making friends with the women won't get you anywhere," I said. "They can't give you Fortitude."

"Of course, they can't," she replied. "But women know things. Women see and hear things men think they're too stupid to understand."

A slow smile spread across my lips.

"Little birds know when to stick together," she murmured. "A flock of sparrows is more powerful than a single hawk."

"Your father is watching," I said. "We're walking a fine line."

"He gave you the attitude speech as well, huh?" She snorted and shook her head. "After all this time... Coming face to face with him..." She plucked at a strand of her long, chestnut hair and twirled it between her fingers.

I watched the movement, my hand tightening around the liquor bottle. That was when I saw the mark on her thumb—the same mark that was on mine.

"What the hell is this?" I hissed and grabbed her wrist. "You let them *brand* you?"

Sloane wrenched her arm away and glared at me. "It was Marini," she spat. "He manipulated me into it. I couldn't refuse, not if I want to keep playing the game. My association with him is the only chance I've got."

She was right, but I didn't like it. A woman would never lead the pack, but a Marini could—*a Marini who could turn at will.*

"You're not having second thoughts, are you?" she asked.

I shook my head. "I can't. Not if I want my freedom. If I'm forced to remain, then I will turn off my humanity again...and I... I can't go through this again."

She took a step towards me. "Does it hurt?"

I grimaced and downed some more alcohol. "I don't like them hurting you."

"We're not going to come out of this unscathed. You know that." She stepped forwards, closing the distance between us. If we were caught together, Marini would put a bullet in me on the spot, and when I woke, he'd do it again.

"Sloane..."

She threw herself into my arms and caught my lips with hers. A rush of desperate need overcame me, and I kissed her, claiming her mouth and fisting my hands into her hair. Twisting my fingers, I tilted her head to the side and deepened my hold, plunging my tongue against hers.

There was something else happening between us.

Something...

Something forgotten.

I tore myself away and cursed under my breath. *Damn humanity.*

"We can't," I said, even though I wanted nothing more than to hold onto her.

"I need you," she whispered. "I'm not afraid of it anymore."

It was a rare thing for her to admit, much like it was for me. Had I told her that? Probably not. I never told anyone anything.

It was a long moment before the air cooled between us.

"Marini didn't tell you what he plans to do with me, did he?" Sloane asked.

"No."

She sighed and lifted her hand, tilting her thumb back and forth. "It's healed already."

I frowned. "Keep it hidden for a few days."

Her gaze met mine and I knew I'd lingered too long.

"I'll be watching," I murmured, reaching for the lock on the door.

"Chaser?"

I hesitated, glancing over my shoulder. I wished we were still on the road and this was another motel room. I wished I wasn't bound to the pack.

She smiled. "Don't do anything stupid, okay?"

"No," I whispered, "I won't."

CHAPTER 7
SLOANE

My first kiss with Chaser wasn't how I'd envisioned it going down. Honestly, I wasn't sure it'd ever happen. For one thing, I'd had a hard time admitting 'caring' meant something closer to 'loving,' not since I saw the photograph of Loretta—the woman he'd loved a hundred years ago.

The woman he'd *married*.

Three whole days of testing the Fortitude boundaries had passed, and I was still no closer to finding out what Marini planned to do with me, or made any headway with the pack, but at least I was still breathing and vampire sightings had been down to a single, fleeting, clandestine meeting.

Sam had taken her responsibility of looking after me a little too seriously. I hadn't had another run-in with Harley, my father had seemed to have forgotten all about me, and Chaser had disappeared.

They were all absent, apart from Sam, but I wasn't naïve enough to think I wasn't being watched. I wanted to give the timid blonde the benefit of the doubt, but I knew she was easily manipulated. The poor woman was squashed under Harley's thumb so hard, she was borderline broken. The only eyes I could trust belonged to Chaser.

I was marked now, but it wasn't a one-way ticket into the pack. It was a mark that branded me as Fortitude property, not that I belonged.

I hated to say it but I was getting lonely, and it'd only been three days. What did that say about me, I didn't know. But I knew I missed Yvette's fashion advice. I even missed Bobby the bald bouncer's unquestioned protection and the fisticuffs from the *Sailor's Arms* upstanding clientele.

Most of the wolves had kept a wide berth, probably at Marini's order, but when I walked towards the exit that led to the garage, no one stopped me. Not like they had when I'd tested the doors elsewhere in the compound, when I'd been greeted with a wall of wolf and shoved back inside every single time. The garage seemed to be an okay place to go...and that worried me.

The scent of grease and exhaust fumes filled my nostrils as I entered the workshop.

It was a hive of activity. Music blared from speakers set into the roof, a car was hoisted up into the air while another was on the ground next to it, and a row of motorcycles sat against the wall beside me. On the far side was a large room that looked like it was used for spraying paint and detail, and an office sat at the front by the double roller doors.

The entire place was painted with a tattoo-inspired mural, which had me thinking of Ratchet. Fortitude Customs was written in script while colourful flames, a skull, and a not-so-subtle wolf made up the bulk of it.

I recognised Spike, glimpsing him before he rolled underneath the chassis of the car he was working on. Glancing around at the other faces, I jerked to a halt when I saw a familiar face.

Gasket.

The old man was on his knees, working on a motorcycle and hadn't seen me yet. I stared, my heart racing.

He was greyer than I remembered. His slicked-back hair and full beard were silver with flecks of dark chestnut, and his face was hard and weathered. Paired with his broad shoulders, ripped torso, and thighs the size of tree trunks, the hair colour seemed to be the only thing that *had* changed.

My mind conjured up childhood visions—him and my mother, his hand ruffling my hair, a present he'd brought me on my birthday, hushed words behind closed doors. Now that I knew what Fortitude really was, I began to wonder what his role in our lives had really been.

I'd always through he and my father were best of

friends, but after my mother died, he'd disappeared along with Marini. If anyone was going to come and see me, it would've been Gasket, but he'd disappeared and I'd forgotten all about him. It wasn't worth remembering—not then, *but now...*

Crossing the garage, I stood next to him. I kind of got why he never sought me out, considering the politics in this place were screwed up to the extreme, but the pack rule book didn't forbid *me* to make contact.

He glanced up at me, sensing I was looming over him. "Well, ain't you a sight for sore eyes."

"Is that all you've got to say to me?" I demanded.

Gasket stood, towering over me, and wrapped his arms around my shoulders. "It's good to see you, kid, though I wish it were under better circumstances."

"You and me both," I replied, pulling away. He still smelled like spice, though it was now laced with motor oil and the distinct scent of werewolf.

"Never thought I'd see you again." His eyes sparkled. "Thought you'd gone off and started some new life far away from this shit."

I didn't want to have 'the conversation' about what had happened to me in the last two weeks, let alone the last fifteen years—and especially not in front of the other wolves. Gasket knew what was going on. He had to.

I narrowed my eyes as he stared down at me. Silent

challenges flew between us and I snorted. "You've got some serious explaining to do."

"There's nothing I can say that you don't already know," he told me.

It was yet another lie the pack was feeding me, and I didn't like it. Anger welled up inside me and I turned away, squashing it down.

"B—" Gasket coughed. "Sloane—"

"What are you working on?" I interrupted.

"I'm tuning the engine on this hunk of junk."

"How do you do that?" I asked, kneeling beside the motorcycle.

The air seemed to clear between us—a silent werewolf truce that filtered through the entire garage —and I sensed the eyes watching us turn away.

"What? You want to get your hands dirty? With pretty fingernails like those?" Gasket grinned and shook his head.

"Got nothing else to do." I made a face. "You know full well I've been ordered to stay put. There's only so much I can take."

I turned my attention to the motorcycle. It was a pretty thing, all black and chrome. It was understated and not as big and bulky as the bikes lined up outside.

"What's this part?" I asked, tapping the side underneath the handlebars. It was painted a shiny black with the model of the bike written on it in fancy lettering.

"That's the fuel tank," Gasket replied. "Here."

Standing, he pointed out the different parts—the radiator, muffler, oil tank, shock absorbers, the engine casing, breaks, ignition, and clutch. There wasn't much to it, but I had no idea what to do with a muffler.

"It's a nice motorcycle," I said. "But it's a lot smaller than the others. They're all beefed-up tricycles."

"Tricycles?" one of the wolves called out. "Watch yourself, Sloane!"

Gasket snorted, covering up a smile. "Most of the men around here like their motorcycles big and sounding bigger."

"Is it a dick thing?"

"A big dick thing!" Spike shouted from under the car, causing a roar of laughter to echo through the workshop.

"It's Chaser's," Gasket said, watching me closely. "I hope he treated you good. He's got a reputation, and it ain't sunshine."

"As well as can be expected when a bunch of fruitcakes are shooting at you," I said, not letting the mention of his name show on my face.

Gasket snorted, not looking too pleased.

So this was Chaser's bike. Now that I knew him better, something classic and simple suited him down to the ground. The vampire wasn't showy, he just got the job done.

"I expected something...meaner," I said, curling my lip.

Spike appeared on the other side of the bike and

snorted. "Chaser's a pretty boy. Pretty boys need pretty bikes."

Gasket raised his eyebrows ever so slightly but said nothing.

"So, what are you doing to it? Giving it a tune-up or something?" I asked, steering the conversation away from dangerous waters. Rock the boat too much and I might get flustered and give myself up.

"Right on the money, sweets."

"He hardly rides," Spike said. "It's a wonder it ain't rusted through."

"Oil, radiator, brakes, tire pressure, engine." Gasket tapped each part as he rattled off his mental checklist. "You want to learn or something?"

"Can I?" I tilted my head to the side. It wasn't bartending or studying to become an educated whatever, but it was something to do and a way to get closer to the wolves I wanted to win over.

Spike snorted and walked away, giving his verdict on the subject. Obviously, he thought I was joking.

Gasket narrowed his eyes and sighed, knowing full well what I was like. "C'mere."

Smiling, I knelt beside him as he got back to work, telling me all the ins and outs of the engine. He handed me a spanner and got me tightening nuts and bolts so I could pretend I was actually helping. It was quite charming...if I were five years old.

"What the hell happened to you?" Spike exclaimed, his voice echoing over the music.

"I got a talkin'-to, that's what happened." *Ratchet.*

"For what?" Gasket rose to his feet, the tenor changing in his voice. One minute he was all fatherly and sweet, and the next, his big bad wolf was switched on. It was slightly terrifying.

Turning, I swallowed a gasp as I saw the swollen blob that was Ratchet's eye socket, and I knew.

Marini.

Ratchet glared at me with his one good eye and said nothing. He knew he'd been played, used as a pawn in a game no one knew the rules to but the alpha.

I opened my mouth, but before I could say anything, Gasket grabbed my wrist and pulled me away from the engine. I dropped the spanner and it clattered to the concrete, the metallic clang echoing through the garage.

"Betty," he exclaimed when he finally saw the tattoo on my thumb. *The tattoo that'd already healed.* "What the hell are you doing?"

"Don't call me Betty," I snapped, wrenching away from him.

"What are you trying to do? Get yourself killed?"

"You think this was me?" I hissed. "You think I wanted this? This was Marini. He ordered Ratchet—"

He wrenched me closer. "*Shut your mouth.*"

"Get your hands off me." I couldn't pull away. If I did, I'd out myself as a full-time wolf. Gasket seeing the healed tattoo was already too much.

"Don't be stupid, Sloane. I remember your mother. She was the most intelligent woman I ever met. *Be like your mother.*"

"Don't talk about my mother."

"There's more going on here than you realise," he whispered. "*I'm trying to help you, girl.*"

My eyes widened and I relaxed as his grip loosened.

"Watch your footing," he went on, raising his voice so the others could hear. "*All* of you. You know what Marini is like."

Spike snorted and I glanced at him, aware everyone in the garage was listening to our conversation. Ratchet continued to glare at me like a sullen child.

"He can't do this," I said to him. Marini wasn't going to own me, let alone scare off every single wolf in this place—it was counterproductive to my secret plan for domination.

"What are you going to do, huh?" Ratchet asked, curling his lip. "He's alpha."

I couldn't do anything, and everyone knew it. To them, I was just a human playing a werewolf's game. I had no power here.

"You'll see," I muttered, turning my back on him. "*You'll all see.*"

CHAPTER 8
SLOANE

It was quiet in the compound.

Marini had beaten Ratchet for tattooing the pack logo on my thumb. The mark that signified I was property...the tattoo he'd ordered to be put there.

He was sending a message, one that'd been received loud and clear. *The alpha's daughter was off limits.*

I didn't want to believe it, but there was a minuscule part of me that'd hoped I was back because he wanted his daughter in his life. That this wasn't about his pride or a shady blood sacrifice or even about power. Who wanted to follow an alpha who couldn't control his own flesh and blood?

Holding up my hand, I stared at the tattoo. The same crossed swords that some past alpha-hole had tricked Chaser into being branded with. I wanted to throw up.

"What did I tell you?"

The sound of an enraged male voice tore me from my self-pity party, and my head jerked toward the direction of the common room.

"Stupid bitch."

The sound of something crashing and a pained wail drew me forwards. I powered down the hall and into the common room. Screeching to a halt, my mouth fell open as I took in the scene before me.

Sam was on the ground, blood welling from a cut on her lip, and her face was stained with tears and smeared mascara. Harley stood over her, his fist raised and his face contorted with rage.

My heart twisted, painfully scraping at the sides of my chest cavity.

I watched Sam lying there, with Harley dominating her like a rabid beast, and I saw red. I sucked in a deep breath as a chill passed through me.

I saw Harley towering over Sam and it was *her*. It was my mother.

Harley had manipulated her good nature. He'd used her as a punching bag, abusing her emotionally and physically. He revealed in dominance and fed off violence. And it didn't matter who it was, as long as he was in control of their terror. Why? *Why?*

The same thing Marini had done to my mother.

I didn't think, I just flew into action.

My vision was tinted red with rage as I strode into the room.

I grabbed the pool cue off the table and held it high. "Get the hell off her!" I roared.

Harley's gaze snapped to mine and his lip curled. The look in his eyes should've given me pause, but I didn't give him the satisfaction of looking away. I didn't even blink as he attempted to intimidate me with his sheer size.

"What you goin' to do with that?" he asked with a sneer.

"Get away from her," I said again.

"She's *mine*. That means I get to do what I want with her, and there ain't nothin' you can do to stop me."

My fingers tightened around the pool cue, and I swallowed the knot of rage that was threatening to take my control. *The wolf within was waking up...*

"Sloane."

Harley's attention shifted at the sound of Gasket's voice, and I struck. I kicked the wolf between the legs, the toe of my steel-capped boots colliding with his crotch. He doubled over with a cry of pain, and I cracked him on the back of the skull with the pool cue. Then I brought up my knee, slamming it into his face.

Harley groaned and blood dripped onto the concrete floor from his nose. I stepped back, a wickedly satisfying grin pulling at my lips. I was starting to understand what it meant to be part wolf. The snowballing of my transformation was triggering new sensations—sensations that should've frightened me but didn't. They were *natural*.

"*Bitch!*" Harley exclaimed. "*You broke my nose!*" He lunged at me, his face crimson with rage.

I could see Gasket in my peripheral vision, readying himself to launch onto Harley, but I didn't need him to fight my battles.

Not now, not ever.

Swinging the pool cue, it rapped him on the ear, and he slipped on his own blood and fell on his side. *Hard*.

I could've walked away from this. I could've kept my nose out of other people's business and continued with my plan for low-key infiltration, but I just couldn't. Not when I saw a man beating up on a woman, and not when I could do something about it.

Leaning over him, I resisted the urge to spit in his face. "If you touch her again, I'll break more than your nose."

"*Sloane*," Gasket barked, the tone of his voice ordering me to stand down.

Reluctantly, I tossed the pool cue aside and backed off before I stabbed it through Harley's eyeball. He deserved worse. *Much worse*.

"Watts, get Butcher," Gasket went on, handing out instruction to the audience I wasn't aware had gathered for Harley's smackdown. "Rhodes, get a mop and haul Harley's ass off the floor. Enough humiliation has been handed out for one day."

That was considered enough? That was a drop in the ocean.

I dabbed a cotton bud on Sam's lip and she hissed.

"That stings," she said with a sniff.

"Of course, it stings," I shot back. "That means it's working."

After I threatened Harley, I hadn't waited around to see them drag him off the floor. Instead, I'd hauled Sam to her feet and got her out of there. We were now in my room. She was sitting on the end of my bed while I attempted to clean her up.

"You shouldn't have done that," she said, her eyes welling with tears.

"There was no way in hell I was standing by and letting him hit you."

"He's a werewolf, Sloane..." she told me. "He could've killed you."

I grimaced. I hated lying to her, especially now. "I don't care what he is, and I don't care that I'm human... and it especially doesn't matter that he's a wolf. He shouldn't treat you like that."

"I know what he is," she murmured. "But...I'm trapped."

"Why?" I asked, my brow furrowing. "Why do you say that?"

Her gaze lowered. "You don't understand."

She was right. I didn't understand. I'd always been strong and not afraid to speak my mind. I'd always stood up to men who tried to dominate me. Marini, Chaser, the unsavories who frequented the *Sailor's Arms.* I'd never thought twice about protecting myself, so Sam was right. I didn't understand, and I probably never would.

I could try to help her all I liked, but she had to *want* my help for it to mean something.

Sam was just one of many in this place. The stronger women—like Shondra, Raquel, Kelly, and Emily—were werewolves. They knew how to get by in a world driven by pack rules, but not Sam. Her humanity and her sweet, loving nature let her down time and time again.

I couldn't help everyone, not if I wanted to take over Fortitude and use the pack to go head-to-head with the Hollow Men. Revenge was a dish best served cold, but it took an army to prepare a meal the size Chaser and I needed. Helping Sam might jeopardise everything.

Maybe I should just kill Marini and get the hell out of here. Maybe that was enough for now. We could get to the Hollow Men another way. Helping Sam was the right thing to do.

"Why?" she asked, turning my question back to me. "Why would you help me? I don't even know you."

Lowering my hand, I tossed the cotton ball into the

bin and sighed. "When I walked in, I saw you lying there...but it wasn't you."

"What?"

"Marini used to beat my mum when I was a kid," I said. "She tried to hide it from me...she would send me away so I wouldn't see, but kids are smart. I knew what he was doing to her. I was too little to stand up for her, but I can stand up for you now."

Sam wiped her tears and glanced at the door.

"That's awful," she said, her entire demeanour changing. "I'm sorry that happened to her, but I'm not your mum."

She stood and crossed the room, leaving me by the bed.

"If you want help, I can give it to you," I said. "All you have to do is say the word."

She turned, a smile plastered on her battered face —a smile that never reached her eyes.

"Harley loves me," she declared. "He'll protect me. Don't worry, Sloane. Everything will be okay. You'll see."

Then she left.

CHAPTER 9
SLOANE

When I needed Chaser's reassurance, he was nowhere to be found.

But that was the life we'd signed up for when we decided to come back to Fortitude. Scratch that—it was my idea. I'd forced him to come along for the ride, and now I was in trouble. *Big trouble.*

I'd come in here with my bravado and newly awakened werewolf powers, but I couldn't let go of my feminist ideals long enough to grasp the bigger picture. Instead of saving one life along the way, I might save them all.

When Harley turned up with a sticky plaster across his nose and two black eyes , it wasn't as satisfying as I'd hoped. There was murder in his eyes, and it was aimed directly at me.

Chaser said he would keep watch over me, but I hadn't seen him in days. Not fighting by his side was hollow. It was strange how much he'd come to mean to me in such a short amount of time...and how starkly I felt it when he wasn't here.

Chaser didn't give me courage—only I could do that—but the thought of us being together at the end of all this, *free*...well, that was something to be courageous for.

"Your father wants you to have dinner with him."

I glanced up at Gasket and scowled. It was so freaking hot, the leather sofa in the common room was sticking to the backs of my thighs. I'd forgotten how sweltering Melbourne could be when it turned up the heat.

"Someone really needs to work on the air conditioning in this hole," I said, trying to ignore the part where Gasket said the words 'father' and 'dinner' in the same sentence. I knew I was going to get a talking-to over my various indiscretions over the past few days. Thinly veiled threats were Marini's way of showing his love, after all.

"He's not going to do anything to you." Gasket sat beside me, the sofa dipping under his weight.

"I was just trying to help her."

"You made it worse, you know," Gasket said. "And for you, too."

"You're saying I should've let him hit her?"

"Harley would've got his eventually, but not like this," the wolf replied.

"What's that supposed to mean?" I demanded. "Were you—"

Annoyingly, we were interrupted before the insults began to fly.

"Betty."

"*Don't call me Betty*," I snarled as Rick appeared like a creeper, rubbing salt into one of my many open, festering wounds.

"Go with him, girl," Gasket said. "It'll be worse if you don't."

I followed Rick in sullen silence. It was hard for me to remember this place wasn't a democracy.

Whatever happened in that room, I was going to hold my own. I had to tell myself I was more valuable to the pack alive than dead. While I drew breath, I had a chance of escape.

I'd gotten out of worse situations. *With Chaser's help*, a little voice inside me taunted. *You never got out of anything yourself. Even when you turned, you still got caught and got Chaser killed. It was all your fault.*

Rick opened the door to Marini's rooms and glared at me. He was styling himself as an alpha-in-training, and it rubbed me the wrong way.

I said a little prayer and stepped inside, hoping Marini had left his pretty mother-of-pearl revolver on the coffee table where I'd last seen it...unloaded.

But I was greeted with exactly what Gasket had said my father had wanted me for. Dinner.

The table was set, and two meals were waiting—steak, vegetables, and roasted potato. How...*homely*.

Marini was waiting, already seated at the table, with a bored expression on his face. Leaning back in his chair, he waved me into the room, exasperated at my obvious reluctance to be in his presence.

Rick slid out the chair opposite and glared at me. Apparently, he didn't like being designated waiter for the evening.

I sat, my gaze raking over the table, taking in the splendour of werewolf-made food and canned beer before settling on Marini.

He sat at the end of the table, stroking his beard like a slimy predator, his wicked eyes watching me, watching him. Finally, he lifted a hand and dismissed Rick, who sneered and strode from the room.

I eyed the new recruit and rolled my eyes.

"He's green," Marini said. No hello, no how are you doing, just straight into it.

"I'm sure he didn't expect to be your slave when he signed up," I replied, not skipping a beat.

My father smirked, the action letting me know my passive-aggressive insult hadn't flown over his head.

"What do you want, Betty?" he asked, reaching for his beer. "Other than making enemies everywhere you go. Harley had a good beating coming to him, and quite frankly, it was overdue, but not from you."

"A woman can't beat on a man who deserves it around here? I thought the strong prevailed, *Daddy*."

"Sam is Harley's property, not yours."

"*What?*"

"Pack rules. I wouldn't expect you to understand, being human and all." He tilted his head to the side. "So, what is it, Betty? What do you want?"

"I made it clear what I wanted the first night I came in here," I replied, my sneer matching his. "*Crystal* clear." He sipped his beer, making a horrible slurping noise that made my stomach churn. *Ugh.* I wouldn't be surprised if it were brewed with the tears of his victims' families. "After what you put me through, I deserve it."

Marini slammed the can down. Reaching over the table, he grabbed my hand and wrenched me close. The force jolted the table, knocking over the glass of water in front of me. The liquid spread, but I hardly noticed. My gaze was locked on my father's face with laser point accuracy.

His smile had faded, and he'd taken on a demonic look. I remembered it well enough when his fist was raised in the air, ready to fly at Mum's face. I imagined this was the look he got when he faced his enemies.

His eyes were wide and his lips thin with anger as he twisted my wrist. Pain shot up my arm, but I wouldn't allow him the satisfaction of seeing me squirm—or the satisfaction of forcing me to reveal myself. I let him hold me, steeling myself for the threat that was about to slap me around the face. Metaphorically speaking, of course.

"Don't think I can't see what you're doing, Betty," he

said, taking manic to a whole new level. "Taking women away from deserving men, interfering with their business, making *friends*. If I don't kill you, one of them will, and I didn't go and get you for nothing."

"You went and got me?" I asked, sneering. "You sent your token vampire to do what you should've done years ago. You did nothing but sit on your putrid throne and bark orders."

"You don't need to fight anyone's battles, Betty," he said, pulling me closer. "No one takes aim at you. Stay out of Harley's way and stay out of pack business."

"Or what? You'll beat them up like you did Ratchet? The wolf you ordered to tattoo me?"

"Is that what he told you?"

I snorted at the blatant lie and wrenched my wrist away.

He was just humouring me. Lulling me into a false sense of security so I would feel safe. Then, once he'd won me over with his psychotic threats, he wouldn't blink when he had to sacrifice me for his own personal gain.

I couldn't let him know I knew what he was up to. I couldn't let him know I was more than human. I couldn't let him know that I knew all about the Hollow Men and their blood sacrifice. I had to play along, no matter how sick it made me feel.

"What do you want with me?" I asked, turning down the anger in my voice. "Tell me. It's obvious you don't want me to be part of your *family*. Just don't tell me the things I've done to get here have been for nothing."

Marini leaned back, his face returning to its usual passive state.

"They had me," I went on. "The Hollow Men had me until Chaser busted in and killed them all. I could be hanging from their king's ceiling right now. I could be dead like—"

"*Shut your mouth.*"

What? So now he cared about what happened to Mum? *Fat chance.*

"What are you going to do about them?" I asked, sticking my finger right into the open wound. "How long am I going to be locked up here?"

"As long as it takes." He rubbed his hand over his beard and snorted. "You're a real pain in my arse. A real pain."

I shrugged. "I'm a Marini. *It's in my blood.*"

He snorted again and picked up his beer. Looking at the food in front of me, I realised I'd lost my appetite and wondered how well it would fly if I asked to be excused.

I stood and glared at him with all the hate I could muster.

"Sit. *Down*," he said, the threat clear.

I swallowed hard as my backside hit the chair.

"Being my daughter is not a one-way ticket. People earn what they have around here through blood. You haven't earned anything, Betty."

I glanced at the steak, which was getting colder by the second like some kind of screwed-up metaphor.

"Then what do I do?" I asked. "Just sit around and twiddle my thumbs?"

"Gasket said you showed interest in the garage. Why, I don't know, but if you must do something, help him. What I don't need is a vigilante getting herself beaten up or worse. If you have to take your PMS out on something, take it out there, not on Harley's face."

My heart took flight. Gasket was respected around here. If I fell in with him and the wolves in the garage, there was a good chance for a do-over. I'd come in guns blazing and cocky as hell. Obviously, that hadn't gone so well with the enemies I'd already made, but getting myself a gig as a mechanic's apprentice could be something. More people looked up to Gasket than Marini, and he'd said he was trying to help me.

Maybe I could trust Gasket, even though he wasn't telling me the entire truth. *Maybe...*

"Eat your dinner, Betty," Marini ordered. "Don't let good food go to waste."

Smirking, I picked up my knife and fork, the passive-aggressive insult hitting home. I'd been thrown a bone, but I knew the next time I overstepped the line, I wouldn't get off so easy. No more beating up werewolves or next time, it would be me writhing in pain on the floor, no matter how valuable I was.

Message received, loud and clear.

CHAPTER 10
CHASER

I t's about time, don't you think?

Staring at the photo of Loretta I kept in my wallet, I thumbed the bent corner.

It might've been a hallucination compounded by the bullet to the heart and the resulting desiccation, or her ghost *had* visited me. There was no way of knowing for sure.

She'd been real enough but letting go was hard... and developing feelings for another woman was even harder. My humanity was a tenuous thing to begin with.

Taking Fortitude was what Sloane wanted, but I had my doubts. I admitted the impossible after what happened on the train. That I cared about her. That I was ready to move on from what had been taken from me with Loretta. I knew what we were getting ourselves into by coming back to Fortitude, but the reality was different than what I was expecting.

Being apart from her... It was tough. It was tougher admitting it, too.

The lights of Melbourne spread out before me, the skyscrapers shining so bright they dulled all but the brightest stars in the sky. Below, I could hear the music and ruckus from the yard behind the compound. The scent of grilling meat wafted up in the sweltering air, calling out to my empty stomach. I was starving, but not for human food, and certainly not enough to leave my sanctuary on the roof. No one came up here, which made it the perfect place for me to separate myself from my sentence downstairs.

Leaning back against the air-conditioning stack—which didn't work, and Marini was too cheap to pay to get fixed—I picked up the can of beer beside me and downed a mouthful. It was warm but better than nothing when my throat burned for blood.

The roof door screeched as it opened, and I slid the photo back into my pocket.

Glancing up, I saw Gasket had found his way to my hiding spot. The old man was a fixture of level-headed composure around these parts.

The only reason he was up here was that he had something he needed to hash out with me. We weren't the best of friends. We didn't hang out. We didn't chat over a beer. We didn't *anything*. Whatever he had to say was about pack business, meaning Marini must have a job for me.

"How's the desiccation?" he asked, standing over me.

"Gone," I replied. "I'm a fast healer."

Gasket snorted and sat beside me, leaning against the air-conditioning stack. He screwed up his face as he settled. "I'm getting too old for this shit," he muttered, rubbing his knee.

"What do you want, Gasket?" I asked, curling my lip.

"I'm worried about Sloane." He shook his head. "She was always Betty, and now she calls herself Sloane."

"And why do you think I care?" The words tasted like acid, but this was the game she wanted us to play. She promised me freedom, and I promised I would watch over her. The trick was getting the old man to talk without catching on to the fact I wanted to know about Sloane's comings and goings. *If only I could compel other supernaturals.*

"That girl was always like a daughter to me," he said. "After her mother was murdered, she latched onto me for better or worse. She had no one else. Broke my heart to send her away. Now... I don't know who she is now."

"Couldn't say," I replied blandly. "Two weeks on the road with her was enough for me."

"Two weeks in a life-and-death situation?" He

raised his eyebrows, waiting to see if I would take his bait. He really should know better by now.

"It's my job." I held up my hand so he could see the brand. "It's not like I had a choice."

"You took a wooden bullet to the heart for her."

I glared at him. "So?"

He snorted and shook his head, turning to stare out at the Melbourne skyline. *What a hole.*

I was sure there were good people out there, but with the way the world was these days, it was every man for himself. Even for the people who actually paid their taxes and had perfect little houses with picket fences. Loretta always wanted to live in a little seaside cottage in Devon, back in England, and I would take her past the houses by the water so she could dream her dreams, but we'd never quite got there. I didn't know what Sloane wanted, but maybe that was a good thing. No expectations.

"She's gone and got herself tattooed," Gasket went on. "Went and beat up Harley, too. Broke his nose. There's a lot of strength in her arm... I wonder why?"

My face twitched. There was no way he missed it.

"I'm going to be straight up with you, Chaser."

"Here we go," I drawled.

"You care about her," he declared. "You and her... More happened out there than you've admitted. More than she's let on, too."

I snorted and downed another mouthful of beer. Gasket liked to think he was observant, but he knew nothing. I didn't care what his relationship with Sloane was, but what was between us was not for him to know. Not when she was locked up inside the compound, surrounded by an entire pack of werewolves.

"I think you told her about her blood. I think you told her about the pack. I think you told her about the vampires." He narrowed his eyes. "And I think you let her turn."

My hand tightened around the beer can, the pressure crinkling the flimsy aluminium. "You think a lot of nonsense, old man."

"You might think you've fooled Marini, but it's only a matter of time before he sees right through you."

"The man isn't capable of love, so even if it were true, he wouldn't be able to work it out," I shot back.

"You used to be such a good liar," Gasket remarked, tilting his head towards the sky. "A real manipulator. After the Hollow Men killed your wife, the only thing I thought you cared about was revenge. A century is a long time waiting."

"Don't you dare talk about her," I snarled. "You don't get to. Understand?"

He brought his chin down and stared me right in the eye. "Is that what you told Sloane?"

I ground my teeth.

"Does she feel the same way?"

I said nothing.

"Your humanity is coming back, isn't it?"

"*Will you shut the hell up?*" I barked.

"For now, she reeks of vampire, but it's only a matter of time before the entire pack smells it on her," he went on. "You're playing a dangerous game, Chaser. Who do you think Marini will believe if it comes down to it?"

I narrowed my eyes. I wanted to say it was me, but Gasket was childhood friends with Marini. His family had been part of the pack for generations. I was a century into the game and brought information and skills the old man didn't have, but blood ran thicker than power. Though lately, it was hard to say with the alpha. He lusted after a lot of things that weren't loyal to his oldest brother-in-arms.

"Flip a coin. You'd have better luck working it out," I retorted.

"Right now, she's downstairs having dinner with him. After a week here, he finally wants to see her." Gasket sighed. "And it's not to catch up on fifteen lost years, either."

I glanced at him, my stomach feeling unsettled. It was too soon. Way too soon. She'd stepped over the line with Harley, even though he deserved everything she gave him and then some.

"Why did she attack Harley?" I asked. "Did he try to jump her?"

Gasket shook his head. "No. She walked in on him beating on Sam."

I cursed under my breath. There were so many things wrong with how Harley treated Sam, but interfering was the worst thing Sloane could've done. No one could break a cycle of abuse that deep with one broken nose. Now she was in a room with Marini, getting one of his stock standard talking-tos. There would be no happy family reunion between those two.

"She better watch her back, then," I muttered, crushing the empty beer can in my hand. "Harley won't let this slide. Being Marini's daughter won't stop him."

"I can't watch over her all the time," Gasket said. "This is where I hope I'm right, and you're already looking out for our girl."

"*Our girl*?" I snorted. I used to be so good at reading people, but this old wolf was impossible. If I misjudged, I was as good as strung up. The brand kept me from dying, so I'd suffer a long time being tortured. If he was telling the truth, then the game had turned in our favour. We couldn't afford mistakes.

"For once in your life, drop the tough guy act, Chaser." Gasket's shoulders tensed, and he lowered his chin. "I wasn't able to save her mother, but I was the one who helped her get out...and the one who stopped him from going after her." He sighed. "Until now, anyway. Who do you think convinced him to send you?"

It was my turn to tense up. Gasket had just handed me enough information to get him a one-way ticket six feet under.

"Out there, I can't help her...not with this," he went

on. "On her own, she was done for. They would've gotten to her, and I would be sitting by a grave rather than on this stinking roof with you. In here, I can do something. There is no one else." He eyed me with a look I wasn't sure I could explain. Did Gasket actually trust me with Sloane? The vampire slave? Stranger things had happened.

"Does she know?" I asked, tossing the beer can aside.

"No."

"What about Marini? Does he know it was you who got her out?"

"Not that I know of."

"Are you going to tell her?"

He shook his head. "It's not the right time."

So now we had dirt on each other. It wasn't quite the stuff alliances were made of, but when Sloane's life was at stake, neither of us could take any chances.

"If you care for her like you say, then you'll keep your mouth shut," I said, knowing the game was well and truly up. With Gasket, anyway. "If I need to get her out, I won't be kind to anyone who gets in my way. Not even her surrogate daddy."

"That's all I wanted to hear," the old wolf said with a smirk. "I convinced Marini to let her work with me in the garage. Since she can't leave the compound, I'll be able to watch her there."

"She won't be happy if she finds out."

"I expect she'll be livid." Gasket smiled, showing

me a side I hadn't seen before. He cared. He actually, genuinely cared for Sloane. He wasn't messing around, at least not about this.

I knew Sloane was more than capable of looking after herself. After seeing how she handled things on the road, I believed in her, but the more people we had on our side, the better. Gasket was a good start. He was the beta of the pack, second only to the alpha.

"If Marini does anything to hurt a single hair on her head, I'll kill him myself," I murmured, the threat rolling off my tongue like silk. "I'll kill anyone who tries to stop me and anyone who dares come after us."

"Those are bold words for a vampire bound to the alpha by magic."

"They're true."

"And you'd give up your revenge for her? You'd forget about your wife?"

The photo of Loretta burned a hole in my pocket. I would never stop loving her, but she was dead and buried. There was a point where I'd have to let go and move on. I'd thought I'd done that on the train when I was lying on the floor of that luggage compartment, but here I was, still staring at a creased photograph in the dark.

"Sloane—"

"Wanted a better life," Gasket interrupted. "She obviously saw something in you out on the road. Something you've forgotten. She's a stubborn little upstart, but she doesn't trust just anyone. Look at how she grew up." He gestured at the yard below where the barbecue was still happening. "But you're bound, Chaser. You can't give her what she needs."

"I was supposed to be one of the good guys," I said.

"No one's supposed to be anything," Gasket said. "The world is grey. There isn't any black or white. The only thing that's certain is death...everything else is just a bonus."

I grunted. He was preaching to the choir.

"Be careful what you do next, Chaser," he added, pushing to his feet. "I'll kill you before you hurt a hair on her head."

"What about Marini?" I threw at his back.

"Oh, I'll kill him, too."

CHAPTER 11

SLOANE

S taring up at the popcorn ceiling, I sighed.

Morning light was inching its way through the cracks in the venetian blinds, and the sounds of the city waking up were amplified through the open window. Man, it was hot in here. Hot, sticky, and uncomfortable.

Last night had been awkward as hell. I didn't know who Marini was anymore. I didn't know much about him in the first place, but he'd seemed to have gotten more violent and erratic than ever. I was living easy right now—he'd made that clear and reinforced the fact that I had no power here.

That was where he was wrong. He'd underestimated the Hollow Men, and he'd underestimated me.

I couldn't wait to see the look on his face when he

realised he'd lost his life's work to his daughter. The daughter he was going to sell off for scrap.

Rolling out of bed, I dragged myself into the shower, scrubbing the sleep from my body. I pressed my forehead against the tile and thought about Chaser. If I closed my eyes and thought about it hard enough, I could feel his cold gaze on me.

It was easier to handle being apart from him during the day. Other people were around. But when darkness fell, and I was alone in bed with my own thoughts...that was when I missed him the most.

Today was yet another day we had to spend apart, but it was also a day closer to getting what we wanted.

After I dressed and succeeded in avoiding Sam—I seriously didn't know who was avoiding who after our post-Harley bashing conversation—and scrounged up some cereal in the kitchen, I went out to the garage.

I was on the outs with the other women after the pool cue incident, though I knew it was more to do with their relationships with the pack than it was to do with right and wrong. They gave me the cold shoulder out of loyalty to their alpha, and I couldn't blame them. Survival came at a premium around here.

Standing in the middle of the empty garage, I wiped the back of my hand over my sweaty forehead and breathed in the smell of grease, rubber, and oil. Doing a lap, I examined the car Spike had been working on the other day, had a look over the motorcycles in various stages of their builds, and peered into the room where someone had been spraying metallic red paint onto a pair of motorcycle fenders.

Being a mechanic wasn't exactly what I'd had in mind when I enrolled in university, but it was something. A life skill, you could call it. Everyone should know how to change a flat tire and make sure enough oil was in the engine. And something about radiator fluid. The most I'd ever known was how to fill up the little bottle of water that cleaned the windshield. Besides, who knew how long I'd be here? This seemed to be a great way to integrate into the pack, for better or worse.

"Well, here's a sight for sore eyes."

I turned as Gasket emerged from the office, his muscles accentuated by the loose tank top he was wearing. He'd become ripped in his old age, even more than I remembered. Gasket had always been tough, but he was levelling up to Yoda as more grey appeared in his hair. Why wasn't *he* alpha?

"What brings you out here at this hour?"

"Marini said I could hang out here," I replied. "I know you talked to him about me."

He raised his eyebrows. "You call him by his last name now?"

"It doesn't seem right to call him Dad." I shrugged and glanced around the garage. Chaser's bike was gone.

"Marini sent him on a job last night," the old wolf said, following my gaze.

He sent the vampire away for the full moon, a voice taunted in the back of my mind.

I snorted and turned my attention back to Gasket. "So, what do you want me to do around here? Is this an apprenticeship?"

"You want to be a mechanic now?"

"Life skills." I made the peace sign with my fingers.

"What were you doing before?"

"Working at a pub and going to university on the internet."

Gasket scowled, looking rather disappointed at how average my life had become.

"Gasket, what did you think I went and did? Become an investment banker?" I rolled my eyes.

"What did you do?"

"If you really want to know, I bounced around various shitty foster homes until I turned eighteen. Then I had to live on the street for a year before I got enough cash together to get fake IDs. The last thing I wanted was my father finding me. Then it was another couple of months before I got a job and enough cash to rent my own place."

"I didn't know," Gasket said. "Sloane, if I'd known..."

I narrowed my eyes in warning as the door to the compound opened and one of the wolves walked in.

"Hey, Sloane," Spike said, raising his hand.

I nodded his way and glanced back at Gasket. "So, where do I start...*boss*."

"The office."

"I'm not going to be a pencil pusher," I said with a pout.

"Let her get her hands dirty," Spike said. "That'll be something to see."

"If you want to work in here, you start at the bottom like everyone else," Gasket said like he was delivering a philosophical lesson. Like wax on, wax off from *The Karate Kid*. Striding over to the shelf, he took down a black plastic bottle, a pair of rubber gloves, and a scrubbing brush. Pushing the load against my chest, he smirked.

"What's this?" I scowled at Spike, who stifled a laugh.

"Stuff in here goes on there." Gasket tapped the black bottle, then pointed to an oil stain on the concrete.

The men—who'd multiplied to six by then—laughed as I let out a wail. Knowing this was a test—like when poor kids got sent to the hardware store for left-handed hammers and striped paint—I got to work, dumping some of the solution from the black bottle onto a nasty grease stain. When scrubbing actually worked, I knew there was no such thing as a fake scrubbing brush trick. Not in this garage, anyway.

Losing myself in the task, I thought about Chaser. Where had he gone? What was he doing for Marini?

He hadn't actually gone into any specifics about what he did around here. I'd assumed he roughed up people who'd crossed the pack, but the farther we'd gone on our road trip, the more I suspected it was something more sinister. He was a vampire on a magical leash, after all.

Chaser was a mystery I wasn't sure I would ever completely unravel, but at least I knew where his loyalties sat. Though knowing he was out potentially murdering someone for my father didn't feel nice. It made me positively sick, and it had nothing to do with the chemical fumes, either.

I made it halfway across the garage floor before Gasket relieved me of my duties.

"Go and have some lunch with the boys." Pointing to the sparkling concrete, he added, "You've done a good job."

I sighed and pulled off the gloves. "This apprentice thing is hard work. I can't feel my knees."

"Outside," he said, pointing to the roller door. "And don't try anything, either."

I smiled sweetly and fluttered my eyelashes. "Who, me?"

"Yes, *you*."

Wiping my sweaty hands on my jeans, I wished I had some shorts. The weather seemed to have worsened since yesterday, and the compound was one big, sweltering cesspool of eternal stench. Picking myself up from the ground, I screwed up my face as my joints ached...then eased completely. There were my secret wolf powers again.

Glancing at Gasket in the office, I turned towards the outside world where I could hear the wolves talking and laughing among themselves. Were these guys any different from vampire Bailey, the fake conductor, or any of the vampires who'd hunted Chaser and I on the road? What was I doing?

I closed my eyes and said a prayer, but I couldn't help the image of blood and broken skulls that invaded my mind's eye, and the sensation of every bone in my body breaking...and the freedom I'd felt running across the Nullarbor. The full moon was almost here, and I didn't have to look at the sky to know it.

Outside, a slight breeze had picked up.

"Hey, Sloane," Spike called out. "Wanna beer?"

"Yeah." I walked over to the group of wolves and took the bottle Rhodes offered me.

Rhodes, Watts, and Ram were three guys I'd seen around, but hadn't had the chance to get to know. Not like the others who worked in the garage. Though they'd gotten to see a great deal of my backside today, so there was that.

I sat on a free chair and put on my aviator sunglasses—the ones with the blue lenses I made Chaser buy me way back when all this first began. How long was it now? A month? Time flew and all that.

Watts raised his eyebrows, his gaze going to my

thumb. He was a quiet kind of guy, thoughtful and sharp by the look in his eyes.

Grabbing the bottle opener off Spike, I popped the lid off my beer and took a mouthful. It wasn't that cold, but several degrees south of boiling was better than nothing in this heat.

"Ugh, I forgot how hot it gets here in summer," I said, attempting to get the conversation going again.

"I thought living out west would've hardened you up," Rhodes said, looking me over.

"Who said I was out west?" I made a face and leaned back in the chair, the plastic creaking.

"It's the farthest point away from here," Ram shot at me.

"Whatever." I kicked my feet up on the overturned crate they'd set up as a coffee table. I wanted to ask them questions about the upcoming full moon, but I knew I couldn't, so I complained instead. "I just scrubbed half the garage floor."

"Want a medal?"

"Yeah. A real big one." I smirked and threw my head back with a laugh, causing the other guys to chuckle.

The air was clearer after that.

Ratchet and Butcher appeared, joining the little group, and for the first time, I didn't feel like a prisoner locked away in a hornet's nest. It was a moment of bliss that was short-lived when Butcher levelled his gaze at me and asked about the one thing I didn't want to talk about. *Chaser*.

"What happened out there?" the big beefcake asked.

I tilted my head to the side. "Out where?"

"Chaser got himself all shrivelled up," he said. "Lost a lot of blood. You knew what you were coming back to. Had a chance to ditch the guy, but you scraped his arse off the floor and brought him back here. *Why?*"

"It's like you said. He got himself killed." I stared right back at him, my hand tightening around my beer.

"So?" Ram asked, tossing in his own line of questioning. "Everyone knows you didn't want to come back."

"Everyone knows shit," I snapped. "You know a rumour, Ram."

Butcher nodded in my direction. "Then explain it, Sloane."

"Leave it," Ratchet said with a groan. "What's it matter? She's Marini's kid. Orders are orders. What the alpha says, goes."

"Says the guy who tattooed her and got his face beat in," Spike said with a snort.

"It's no secret my father and I aren't close," I said, picking at the label on the bottle in my hand. "But I am his daughter. Your alpha's flesh and blood...for better or worse."

"You are your father's daughter," Ratchet said,

scowling. The bruise on his eye had faded, his werewolf genes taking care of it.

"I'm also my mother's daughter." I raised my bottle, held it high, and waited.

Ratchet nodded and bumped his bottle against mine. His boldness gave the others courage, and one by one, every bottle clinked against my own. Butcher, Spike, Ram, Watts, and Rhodes.

"*Sloane.*"

Looking over my shoulder, I saw Gasket linger at the garage door. He crooked his finger, calling me inside.

"Boss is callin'," Rhodes drawled.

"I've got another fifty square feet of concrete to scrub," I said with a groan. He was so not calling me inside for scrubber duty, but I thought it best to play coy.

Leaving my empty beer bottle with the wolves, I went inside. The moment we were out of eyesight and earshot, Gasket grabbed my arm and shoved me against the wall.

"Hey!" I exclaimed.

"What are you playing at?" he asked, hissing at me.

"I'm playing at keeping myself alive," I retorted.

"You're *fishing.*"

I made a face. Is that what they called it around here? Fishing for allies in the sewage pipe of life.

"I don't know what Marini's go going on with the Hollow Men, not all of it, but the pack can't help you."

"That's where you're wrong, old man," I said, my anger rising. "Fortitude can help me by me helping Fortitude."

"By taking it over, you mean."

I stared blankly at him but he was far too smart to be fooled by an emotionless stare. He'd been playing this game for his entire life. Playing people, exploiting their weaknesses, beating them, killing when 'reason' didn't get through. Gasket wasn't innocent.

"Stop looking at me like that," he muttered. "I know, Sloane. *I know.*"

Yeah, but how much?

"Marini brought this on me," I murmured, the chill in my voice alarming even me. "The Hollow Men, the abuse, the manipulation...my mother's murder."

"Sloane—"

"Don't you *Sloane* me."

Gasket let go of my arm and ran his hand over his face. Cursing under his breath, he turned away.

"What are you going to do?" I asked his back. "Tell on me?"

He cursed again and faced me, his eyes full of something as far from anger as he could get. Was it regret? Resignation? *What did he know?*

"Even if your father is out of the picture, they'll still come after you," he said. "You know that. It won't end with his death or dethroning."

"Believe me, I know how this works." They all had to go, lest the one left alive out of mercy came back to avenge what they'd lost. I was going for complete and utter annihilation.

"Be careful, girl," the big wolf said. "Be *very* careful."

I nodded, those three words echoing the same sentiments I'd been having since I arrived.

"Sloane..." he trailed off, his expression softening.

"*What?*"

"Full moon's tomorrow night. Best you stay in your room."

My heart leapt. "What happens? Do you remember when you turn?" I rattled off. "Where does everyone go?"

The old wolf's eyes narrowed. "That's not for you to know."

It was, but I wasn't sure I could trust him with that secret, and if I pressed harder, he'd figure it out...if he hadn't already.

"Chaser warned me about wolves, but—"

"Best you keep your mouth shut, too," Gasket interrupted. "And get back to work. That ought to keep you out of trouble long enough to make it to tomorrow."

As he walked away, and the garage fell into silence, I knew I could trust him with my life. Gasket's loyalties would always be with the pack, but that didn't mean they would always be with Marini.

Fortitude was more than just one wolf. *One man.*

It was time for a woman to remind them of that.

CHAPTER 12

SLOANE

The next night, after a long day degreasing the last of the garage floor, I ventured into the Fortitude common room.

I didn't know if it was stupidity that drove my curiosity, but I wanted to know more about what happened during the full moon. Where did the pack go? How did they handle turning?

My own wolf was restless, and it made me fidgety in the worst possible way. As the sun set and night took hold, it only got worse. Was this how the others felt, or was it because this was my first proper full moon since I'd first turned?

Great. I was going through werewolf puberty.

As I waked into the room, I hesitated. It was busier than I had expected. A group of wolves were playing poker at the table in the corner, empty beer bottles piling up around them. They didn't seem in a hurry to clear off, and I frowned.

"Hey, Sloane."

I turned at the sound of Sam's voice and went to sit with her on the couch. I wasn't sure I wanted to be around a bunch of wolves on the precipice of turning. *What if they could smell what I was?* I wouldn't reek of vampire forever. *Damn my curiosity.*

"It's a full moon tonight," I murmured. "Why are they so..."

"Whatever about it?" She smiled and shook her head. "They've been turning since they were teenagers, Sloane. They know when it's time."

"Where do they go?" I asked, glancing across the room to where Spike and Rhodes were arguing loudly over the rules of a royal flush versus a full house.

"Downstairs," she whispered.

"Downstairs? Like in the basement?" I asked. "I have so many questions."

Sam's smile faded. "I wouldn't ask any."

"Why not?"

"They may be used to turning, but it doesn't mean that it doesn't hurt." Her gaze lowered. "Harley says... I asked once..."

My expression softened. I knew what answer she'd gotten. "Forget I asked, then."

As Sam's alarm subsided and her smile widened, I felt a twinge in my chest and grimaced. Something felt off as I curled my hands into fists.

The moon...

Chairs scraped back from the table as the wolves began to move, and I understood. My wolf side was waking up.

"Hey, Sloane," Spike said, looking down at us with narrowed eyes, "you girls staying up tonight?"

"Nope." I shook my head, pushing away the twinge in my chest. "I'm having an early night. All that scrubbing in the garage has got me beat."

Rhodes slapped Spike on the shoulder. "We better get going."

The young wolf gave us one last glance before leaving, his warning clear. Tonight was not a night to go looking for cheap thrills, and for once, I was on the same page.

"I think I'm going to take a shower," I said to Sam. "My back aches like a bitch. All that hunching over and scrubbing has wrecked me."

"Oh..."

I hesitated, even as my wolf raised its head to howl at me. "What is it?"

"I thought you might've wanted to watch a movie or something," Sam said sheepishly. "Harley's gone with the others, and..."

My stomach twisted and I was glad she wasn't big on direct eye contact. "Maybe another night," I told her. "I'd just fall asleep anyway."

"Oh. Yeah, of course..."

I stood. "I'll see you tomorrow?"

Sam nodded, but I didn't stick around to hear her answer.

I couldn't get back to the safety of my own room fast enough. Closing the door behind me, I breathed deeply.

The sliver light of the moon filtered through the window and I tensed, the fluttering in my chest turning into a full on ache. I pressed the heel of my palm against my sternum and rubbed.

"I know you want out," I whispered, "but it's a bad time. I can't reveal you yet."

Pain arced through my body as my inner wolf struggled for control. My bones bent with an unnatural pressure, each one on the verge of snapping, and I fell to the floor, swallowing a surprised gasp.

Chaser said I wasn't tied to the curse of the moon, but what if he and everyone else who believed in my powers were wrong? I could turn any time I wanted, but what if the moon still ruled me?

It's a wolf's nature to answer the call of the moon, I thought as my cheek pressed against the carpet. I dreamed of it constantly—my true nature bound to it, despite being free of the curse. It was my natural instinct to want to change with the pack. That's all this was, right?

I pulled my knees against my chest and breathed deeply. *Don't change, don't change, don't change... That's what Marini wants. He's testing me.*

I shuddered, wanting nothing more than to run

free. To feel the wind against my fur, my paws on the ground, with nothing but the sky above and the night around to comfort me. If I turned, I'd have the pack to run with.

No! The pack didn't know me. They were all locked up. The city was swarming with vampires and humans—it was no place for wolves. I wasn't a Fortitude wolf. Not yet.

I focused on my breathing, remembering when Chaser and I had sat under the stars, watching those vampires burn. It was a twisted memory, but it was the first time I felt close to him, felt his humanity. We had a plan, and if I turned now, it would implode.

Please, I called to the wolf within. *Please don't make me change. We can be together soon... Soon...*

A long, agonising minute passed and finally, the pressure in my bones subsided. The wolf submitted and backed away, disappearing with the light of the moon.

I didn't know how long I'd been laying there, but as my senses returned, I dragged myself into the bathroom and turned on the shower.

All this time, I thought I'd been in control, but the truth was a cruel slap in the face. I was barely holding on—to my plan, to my courage, and to the wolf within. I was arrogant, falling into the same trap that the Hollow Men had laid out for me on that train. Thinking I had all the power when I scarcely had any at all.

Cool water soaked through my clothes, clearing my mind, but not the pull of the full moon.

That was a close call, I thought as I shivered. *Too close.*

Get it together, Sloane.

CHAPTER 13

CHASER

"It's done."

I slammed the revolver onto the table, spinning the butt towards Marini. The mother-of-pearl shone in the light, the beauty of the thing marred by all the lives it'd taken. Instead of a headsman's axe, Fortitude had a gun.

The executioner.

It was late when I'd arrived back at the compound, past one a.m., but Marini wanted an immediate report the moment I got in, whatever hour it was. Revenge, messages, shows of power. Blood never waited, and neither did he.

This time I'd been sent after a wolf who'd fled from the pack only days before. I couldn't blame the guy, but with the Hollow Men watching, the pack couldn't afford any loose ends. One misstep and they'd descend like locusts, kill everyone, and take Sloane. For the first time, Marini and I were on the same page...despite our differing motives.

The dining table in the alpha's room was empty, save for the revolver. Marini sat at the head like he was the king of the world and regarded me smugly. He leaned forwards, his fingers brushing the barrel like a father caressing his newborn child. "And?"

"The vampires hadn't got to him," I replied. "He won't inform on the pack."

"Did you make him squeal?"

I nodded. I'd made it quick and painless, but he didn't need to know that. My tastes had changed in light of certain...*events*.

"Good. What took you so long?"

"I had to make sure there was no heat on him," I said, resting my hand on the back of a chair. "Last thing the pack needs right now is attention."

Marini picked up the gun and turned his gaze on me. "What do you think of Betty?"

"I don't think anything," I replied, unsettled by his abrupt change of subject.

"Yeah, you do think something, Chaser. You think a great deal. It's ingrained in that baby-faced head of yours. You've had over a hundred years to figure out how to hide things from me. I know you do."

I narrowed my eyes. "You ordered me to get her back. I got her back."

"Took you long enough."

"The—"

Marini slammed his fist down on the table, and I was suddenly grateful I'd left the revolver unloaded.

"I don't want your excuses," he snarled. "*Tell me.* What do you think of Betty?"

He was baiting me, which meant he suspected. Whatever I said next, I had to choose my words carefully.

"She may be fighting the wrong battles, but she can fight."

Marini snorted and leaned back in his chair. "And what makes you say that?"

"The Hollow Men," I replied, deadpanning him. "She killed one without blinking. You and I both know how difficult it is...and she thinks she's human."

"Hollow Men..." the alpha scoffed and flipped open the revolver barrel. Seeing the chambers were all empty, he scowled then reached into his shirt pocket.

I stared in confusion as he tossed a broken shard of human bone onto the table. It clattered and slid towards me, a strange shiver rolling down my spine. It had magic in it, I could feel it in the air.

I couldn't take my eyes off it. At five inches long, it had intricate symbols etched into the length to bind whatever spell clung to it. It'd weathered and darkened over the years, the grime of a dozen alpha's settling into the marks. Witches' runes and sigils sealed with blood—a talisman.

"Take it," Marini said, waving absently towards the bone. "Go on."

My gaze lifted to the alpha's.

"What are you so afraid of?" he asked. "Don't you remember?"

I scowled. "Remember what?"

"It's a shard of bone from your own arm," he told me. "I wasn't there, *of course*, but I heard it grew back...*eventually*."

I stared at him in shock, my mind working overtime trying to find the memory...but it wasn't there.

Witches. Had to be. They'd wiped the knowledge from my mind as another layer of protection for the pack. I thought the brand on my thumb was the thing binding me—and no amount of cutting, severing, and scraping had ever removed it. It was as brilliant as it was twisted. If I didn't know the true nature of the spell, then I'd never be able to escape.

"Pick up the bone, Chaser," Marini barked when I didn't move. "Pick. It. *Up*."

The order sank into me, the magic binding the alpha's will to action. I reached out and grabbed the talisman, but the moment it came in contact with my skin, my flesh burned.

Marini smirked, his eyes glinting maliciously as he watched the magic melt my hand.

I grimaced as the pain became unbearable, but I couldn't shut it out. The magic forced me to feel the hold the alpha had over me, to let me know that even though I now knew what bound me, there was no hope. The spell was unbreakable.

I grunted and stumbled against the table, the smell of my cooking flesh filling the room.

"Put it down," Marini said after he was sure I'd gotten the message.

I dropped the bone onto the table and pulled my hand away, hissing as the blistered wound began to heal, but Marini grasped the shard in his hand and squeezed. The pressure bore down on me and my breath caught.

"Don't play me for a fool, Chaser," Marini snarled. "I own you. I own your life. I own your immortality. And I own your *pain*. If you're lying to me, the pain I will cause you will be unbearable, and it will go on for days...weeks...*months*... It will go on for as long as it amuses me." He rounded the table and tightened his hold on the talisman, forcing me to my knees. "*Do you understand?*"

I gasped for air that didn't come. The blood in my veins began to dry and my vision blurred.

Marini loosened his grasp. "Do. You. *Understand?*"

I nodded, coughing as air filled my lungs. "*I understand.*"

The alpha glared down at me, his lip curling, and he slid the talisman into his pocket. "Get up," he snarled. "You're pathetic. A pathetic disappointment. *Get out of my sight.*"

I didn't wait around. I pushed to my feet and stumbled out of the room and into the hallway.

Marini suspected. What, exactly, remained to be seen, but doubt was dangerous enough. I had to warn Sloane to cool off and lay low. Breaking point was never as close as it was right now.

Stopping by the door to the roof, I sighed. The heat, the bloodshed, and Marini's threats were getting to me. My returning humanity wasn't helping, neither was being apart from Sloane.

This shouldn't be hard. Subterfuge was second nature, but the talisman changed everything. It was a part of me, sealed with pack blood. Unbreakable. If I couldn't pick it up, maybe Sloane could. Maybe she could be the one to command me.

But only if she is alpha, a small voice taunted. *Only…*

CHAPTER 14
SLOANE

After I'd finished degreasing the garage floor, I was promoted to repairing punctured tires. It was a step up, and my bruised knees thanked me for it.

Two things that hadn't changed though, were the weather and Chaser's absence. He still wasn't back from whatever awful job Marini had sent him on. I didn't like it, and I'd been dwelling on all the worst outcomes because of it. What if the Hollow Men got him?

I became increasingly irritated with each passing day, and the heat didn't help. The bikers in the garage had started calling me Sulky Sloane until I superglued Ram's arse to a chair.

My fate was still up in the air, and I was still confined to the compound, so all I could do was keep on keeping on. Making friends, skirting around the edges of danger, and avoiding one of my many nemeses—Harley. Sam had started talking to me again, though it was only in one-syllable words, the fear in her voice unmistakable. In the beginning, she'd been ordered to shadow me to glean information, but when I'd taken matters into my own hands, that'd all gone by the wayside. I was now too unpredictable to be around, especially when it came to threatening Harley's domination of her.

Turning over in bed for the hundredth time, I was failing to find a comfortable position. The mattress was lumpy, the air was stifling, and my brain was working overtime.

It was so damn hot in here, sleep was impossible. Sweat stuck to my body as I tossed and turned, the open window doing nothing to ease the heat in the tiny bedroom.

Sitting up, I groaned and rubbed my eyes. *This is impossible.*

Flinging my legs out from underneath the covers, I found my denim shorts and pulled them on, shoved my feet into my boots, and dragged on another T-shirt. Shuffling over to the door, I flipped the lock and peered out into the hallway. No one was standing guard—and they hadn't since I'd arrived—but I wouldn't put it past my enigmatic father to implement it without warning.

Sliding out into the hall, I walked towards the common room, tingling all over like I was doing something naughty. It wasn't against the rules to explore the compound, though I don't know why anyone in my position would want to.

Being the middle of the night, there weren't many people around. I could hear the sounds of men coming and going as I walked the halls, but I saw no one. I found the door to the roof and opened it. No one stopped me. It seemed no one was concerned that I would fling myself off the edge. Glancing once more over my shoulder, I climbed the stairs.

Pushing open the door, a cool breeze wafted into my face, and I sighed. It wasn't much, but it was better than inside. The air was clear, albeit tinged with pollution, and I filled my lungs to the brim before letting it all whoosh out. Total cleanse.

Walking to the edge of the building, I peered over the edge to the concrete below. The roller door was open, and I could hear the sounds of wolves working inside. My enhanced ears picked up on the music blaring from the stereo and the clatter of tools, but the sound covered their conversation.

Edging back from the edge, I looked towards the skyline. Lights stretched as far as I could see, tangerine and white twinkling on a landscape I would never be a part of. All those people with their families, their fame, their mundane jobs, morning commutes, and petty squabbles. What kind of life did I want? Hell if I knew. All I'd wanted was to be somewhere else. Free to figure out who Sloane was in the wake of becoming the world's most wanted wolf.

After the things I'd seen, all I wanted was a future where I was safe. Where Chaser and I were free. That's all I wanted.

I felt Chaser's absence more keenly up here. I wasn't sure why, but it felt like a place he would like. It was away from the chaos downstairs and more in tune with the solitude we'd had on the road. Our world was small then, more manageable. Here, it was too big to keep up with. Whatever happened next, I knew I wasn't made for great things. Small, simple, and quiet, that was where I belonged. Though it kind of went against the whole alpha thing I had going on.

Angling my head towards the sky, I was disappointed I couldn't see any stars. The moon was waning, its presence tugging at the primal instincts inside me, but it was all that was up there. Humanity's mark had invaded the skies.

A hand fisted into the back of my hair and twisted, the abrupt movement taking my breath away. Gasping for air, I cried out as my scalp burned. That was when my fight mode was activated. My body had sensed a threat and lashed out.

I kicked backwards at my assailant, and a male grunt signalled I'd gotten him in the shin. His grip loosened on my hair, and I turned.

Harley.

I knew this moment was coming, but I was hoping it would be later. *Much later.*

The one second it took for me to shake off my

shock was all it took for him to grab me again. He pushed me backwards towards the edge of the roof, and I stumbled and fell. Letting out a scream, the wind was forced out of my lungs as I landed hard, my head hanging over the edge of the building—a hair's breadth away from a three-story drop onto the concrete below

Harley was on top of me, his muscles coiled with the waning strength of the moon, and his hands tightened around my neck. He squeezed, and my fight mode turned into full-blown panic.

"This'll teach you to mess with me," the wolf growled. "Who has the power now?"

I trembled, a sob working its way up the back of my throat, but the hands around my throat caught it.

"No one would ever know it was me," Harley said with a malicious grin. "I could toss you over the edge, and it would look like a suicide."

I clawed at his hands, the broken remains of the acrylic nails Sierra had given me tearing at his skin.

Fight, Sloane! Fight! You're the wolf who can transform at will. You're powerful always. You can win.

"Eat shit," I rasped. "Eat shit and *die*."

I tensed, readying myself to buck with all the energy I had...but his hands slackened, and his head jerked to the side. He fell to the ground, his head cracking on the concrete roof.

Chaser stood over us, his expression full of rage. Deadly, chilling, pulse-pounding *rage*.

Harley didn't get up. He didn't even twitch. His head was at a strange angle, and I knew Chaser had broken the wolf's neck. He'd killed a member of the pack and Marini—

Scrambling away from the edge of the roof, I coughed, my throat scratchy. "What did you do? *What did you do?*"

"I saved your life," Chaser said as I climbed to my feet. "That's what I did."

"What did you do that for?" I shrieked, shoving him as hard as I could.

"What the hell?" His mouth fell open, and he threw his hands into the air. "What's wrong with you?"

"I'm trying to win people to my side!" I exclaimed. "Then you come in and fight my battles. *Mine!*"

He cursed, rubbing his hand over his face.

"I had him," I said, knowing full well there wasn't much truth in that statement. "*I had him.*"

"Me fighting for you is not weakness, Sloane."

"They won't just follow anyone, let alone a woman. I need to give them a reason to follow me."

"By more of the same?" Chaser asked, raising his eyebrows. "By being a bigger maniac than Marini?"

I shoved him, and he stumbled.

"Don't lose yourself to this," he said. "Don't—"

The roar of an engine broke off whatever he was about to say, then an explosion tore through the air, the boom almost knocking us off our feet.

Agonised cries echoed form below and I rushed

towards the edge of the roof. Chaser grabbed my arm, but not before I saw the carnage below.

The charred remains of a car stuck out of the garage door as smoke and flames billowed out of the compound. Men lay prone on the ground, while others crawled outside, their flesh sizzling as they dragged themselves over the concrete.

A car bomb.

"They're burning!" I cried, my nose filling with the sharp scent of burned flesh...and something else. "What the hell?"

"Wolfsbane," Chaser said. "*Poison.*"

A wolfsbane car bomb? It didn't take a genius to put two-and-two together. "*The Hollow Men.*"

"Go back to your room and stay there," Chaser said. "I'll take care of this."

"But—"

"*Sloane.*" He grasped my shoulders. "Vampires can't go inside the compound, not unless they're invited. *Go inside.*"

"What about Harley?"

"I killed him, it's my responsibility." He pushed me towards the door. "*Go inside.*"

I nodded and rubbed at my neck. Moving back into the compound, I was hit with a wall of stifling heat as I hurried through the halls. I was shoved aside by a group of wolves as they barrelled towards the garage, though none of them looked twice at me.

I stared after them, numb. I knew Harley's revenge

and an inevitable play by the Hollow Men was coming. But knowing didn't make it easier to face or to deal with the aftermath.

Turning, I smacked into a hard chest and let out a yelp.

"Steady, girl," a familiar gravelly voice said.

"Gasket."

"What's all the noise?" he asked. "And what are you doing out here?"

"It was a car bomb," I told him. "Drove right into the garage."

Gasket grasped my face in his big hand and tilted my head to the side. "What happened here?"

Twisting away, I scowled. "Harley."

Gasket's expression turned positively demonic. "Where is he?"

"On the roof with Chaser. I think."

"*Shit.*" His expression didn't change as much as I thought it would as he yanked me down the hall to my room. He pulled me inside and closed the door behind us, then grasped my face again. "The marks on your neck are gone, but I already knew that." He wrenched my hand upwards and showed me the tattoo on my thumb. "Just like that, too." His eyes narrowed. "Harley attacks you and now the compound has been bombed. There's been a lot of coincidences lately, huh?"

"You knew, didn't you?" I asked, my heart beating at a thousand miles per hour. "This whole time?"

He grunted.

"*Gasket.*"

He sighed sharply and looked at me. "You think you can rule Fortitude, but it isn't for you, Sloane. Turning doesn't make you an alpha, no matter who your father is."

"You don't know that. It's been a long time since we knew one another."

"If you think you can get away with staging a coup without Marini knowing it's coming, you're in for a rude awakening. My guess is he'll be waiting for you long before you work up the nerve to strike."

I slammed my palm down on his shoulder, forcing him to face me. "He knows?"

"He suspects, which for you is not a good thing right now. Those suspicions could easily turn into something else."

Why hadn't they, then? My mind worked overtime, dwelling on Harley up on the roof and what Marini did or did not know. If he suspected, then why wasn't he acting? Suspicions were usually enough for him to pull the trigger. It could only mean one thing...

My eyes widened. "He's got something planned for me." This was the false sense of security I'd feared all along. I thought I was winning, but in reality, I was the one being manipulated.

"This is not the time, Sloane." Gasket moved around me.

"It never is!"

"The Hollow Men attacked the compound and

there's likely dead wolves out there. When the dust settles, eyes will turn to you. Do you understand?"

I swallowed hard and nodded.

"Stay here," he ordered. "We'll talk about this another time."

"*Gasket.*"

He shook his head. "I'm not askin', girl."

I took a step towards the door, but his glare was enough to put me in place. He'd never looked at me like that before—like he wanted to show me what real discipline was. I wasn't his daughter, but he sure as hell thought I was.

Gritting my teeth, I stayed put. With one last warning glare, Gasket slammed the door closed and left me alone in the safety of his room.

I didn't want a bunch of men running off to my rescue, but here they were doing just that.

CHAPTER 15
CHASER

I lifted Harley's body in my arms and leapt off the roof.

Smoke was pouring from the garage as the car burned and using the confusion to my advantage, I dumped the body near the wreck. Stepping over a wolf writhing on the ground, I ripped off the door and looked inside.

A charred body sat in the driver's seat, the stench of burnt flesh filling my nose.

There was no way it was a vampire—the body wasn't damaged enough for permanent death—it was a compelled human being. *Poor bastard.*

The backseat was wired with spent explosives, wires, and plastic barrels that'd once held litres and litres of a distilled wolfsbane solution. The remains of more containers had melted over the side of the car itself. This thing had been rigged to make one hell of a statement.

"Harley?"

I pulled back, turning to see Spike kneeling over Harley's body. I stood over him and wiped at my nose. It smelt like a rancid, grease-stained barbecue in here.

The wolf looked up at me. "Chaser?"

"The blast must have thrown him against the wall," I said. "He's dead, Spike." I grabbed his shoulders and pulled him to his feet, then pushed him towards the wolf whose flesh was searing with wolfsbane. "Help him. Get him inside and in a shower."

Without another word, Spike hauled the injured wolf to his feet and dragged him inside.

I turned to survey the damage, my gaze raking over the smoking ruin. The entire workshop was damaged, the cars and motorcycles were impaled with shrapnel, and tools and equipment were strewn everywhere.

Snapping into action, I grabbed the nearest able-bodied werewolf, who turned out to be a stunned Ram, and pushed him towards the injured.

"Get your head on," I barked. "Get these men inside and hose them down." I snapped my fingers at another. "*You*, get a fire extinguisher."

As the werewolves came out of their daze, noise filled the garage. Men were carried inside and the *whoosh* of extinguishers filled the space as the fire was put out.

I counted three dead, not including Harley. Wolves I hardly knew, but members of the pack all the same.

The door crashed open, and I turned to see Gasket stride into the garage. His expression turned to thunder when he saw the aftermath of the blast. This wasn't going to be good, but he was the only person I trusted outside of Sloane.

"Gasket." I nodded at Harley's body.

"Don't say another word, Chaser," the wolf growled. "I already saw Sloane. Just tell me, was it you or her?"

"*Me.*"

He hissed. "Bloody hell, Chaser. Does he look like he's been in an explosion to you?"

"Not yet."

"Has anyone seen him?"

I shrugged. "Spike."

Gasket ground his teeth and shoved me up against the wall. "If it wasn't for Sloane, I'd force you to get rid of your humanity," he snarled. "You're getting sloppy, *vampire.*"

"Careful, old man," I murmured. "There's still ears in this garage."

"No, you be careful, Chaser," the wolf warned. "Spike is Marini's."

"It doesn't matter."

He let me go and ran his hand over his face. "*It matters.*"

I grasped Gasket's arm. "Marini threatened me with the talisman earlier tonight. *He knows*."

Gasket gritted his teeth and glanced towards the garage. "We need more time. Sort out the body. Marini will be here any moment."

As the old wolf pulled focus away from me, I found some wolfsbane inside the remains of the car and tore out the melted bottle. Dumping the contents over Harley, I made sure his flesh began to blister before I smeared him with ash. It was a hack job, but it was all I could manage.

Then I called for a wolf to drag him over to the other bodies.

"They'll pay for this!" Marini's voice tore through the garage, his rage pressing down on Gasket and the other wolves on the other side of the destroyed car.

Just in time.

"*Chaser!* I know you're here. I can smell you."

I stepped out of the gloom and saw the alpha had brought an entourage with him. Rocket, Rick, and DeLuca stood behind Marini, their expressions troubled.

"Wolfsbane," I said, dumping the destroyed bottle at his feet. "The car was full of it."

"The driver?"

"Human by the looks of it."

Marini glared at me, his anger affecting me without the added pressure of the talisman. "Cowards," he raged. "They get others to do their work for them. They don't even fight their own battles."

He began to pace, looking at the row of dead werewolves. When he reached Harley, he paused.

I glanced at Gasket, but he wouldn't meet my gaze.

"What do you want us to do, boss?" Rocket asked. "Take the fight to them?"

Marini lingered, his eyes still on Harley. After a moment, he held up his hand. "Not just yet..." He looked at me coolly. "Check the permitter and surrounding streets. If there are Hollow Men out there watching us, I want them found and dealt with."

I nodded and took a step towards the street.

"*Chaser*."

I paused.

"Where's Betty?"

"Inside," Gasket said for me. "I saw her in the hall and told her to stay in her room."

Marini glared at the wolf. "At least someone around here has sense." When no one moved, he shouted, "What are you still standing here? *Go!*"

The wolves scattered and I didn't hang around. I didn't want a talisman repeat, and I definitely didn't want to be there when Marini worked out that Harley wasn't killed by the car bomb.

Out on the street, Gasket fell into step beside me. "Rick."

I saw the outline of the werewolf in front of us and

nodded. If anyone knew what Marini was up to, it was his lap dog.

"It starts now, huh?" I drawled.

Gasket didn't reply. He simply strode up behind Rick and thumped his fist into the back of the werewolf's head.

I sighed. I guessed we were starting now.

We locked Rick in a disused storage closet that'd been converted into a cell. It sat inside the dank depths of the basement and had all the latest modern conveniences. Slate grey feature wall with artful werewolf scratches, white cornices, a rendered concrete bench to sleep on, and a heavy-duty lock on the unbreakable metal door. Conveniently, there was also a drain in the middle of the floor.

Gasket dumped Rick on the bench, and I locked the door behind us. Glancing at the wolf next to me— the man who said he cared about Sloane like a father —I didn't need to explain to him what I was about to do. All he did was nod to let me know we were on the same page.

I grabbed Rick by the scruff of the neck and threw him across the room. He collided with the wall, the bang echoing through the room. The other benefit of being down here, where the wolves turned every full moon, was no one would hear his screams.

Rick was on his feet in a flash, looking for an exit that didn't exist. Tired of his cowardice, I shoved him up against the wall and held my forearm on his chest. Levelling my gaze, I sneered. "You've got a smart mouth on you, huh?"

"Get off me!" He wriggled, but he was no match for my strength.

"What is Marini planning?" I asked, jamming my arm harder against him. "*Talk.*"

"He doesn't tell me anything," he said, snivelling like a little pig. "I just follow orders. Same as you."

"You and I both know I can't compel another supernatural," I said, "but I can hurt you, then heal you...*then hurt you again.*" I inched closer, triumph coursing through my veins as his pupils dilated in fear. "Now...are you going to wet your pants, or are you going to tell me what you know?"

"D-don't kill me," Rick stuttered, showing off what a big man he really was.

Gasket shifted behind me. "Start talking, kid, or this won't end pretty. You know what Chaser is capable of."

Rick was shaking, unable to control his fear. Soon, he'd be catatonic and useless.

"What is Marini going to do to Sloane?" I shook him as my eyes turned back and my fangs began to elongate.

"He's going to give her to them," Rick exclaimed. "To make things go away."

"The Hollow Men?" I growled, my anger turning into something more like rage. After all we'd been through to get here, Marini was just going to give her to them?

"I'm just the messenger," Rick said. "I only follow orders. I deliver letters and stuff."

I grabbed the front of his shirt and jerked him close. "What letters?"

"The witch," he blubbered, his fear sending his heartbeat into overdrive. "I take letters to the witch."

I hissed. "And what are in these letters?"

"*How should I know?*"

"Don't tell me you don't read them before you deliver, because I wouldn't believe you."

"Okay, *okay*." Rick held up his hands. "He's making a deal with the Hollow Men to hand Betty over for the sacrifice, but when he does, he plans to double-cross them."

I shook him. "*How?*"

"By binding King's bloodline with a spell," Rick blubbered.

"Has the deal been made?" Gasket asked, pushing in between Rick and me.

I loosened my grip and stood back, wanting nothing more than to go back to Marini's rooms and put a bullet in his head. He was going to sell off his own daughter in the name of revenge.

Rick shook his head. "Not yet. He's got a witch to

bind the bloodline, but he needs to get inside to make the connection."

It was then that I realised the truth and my stomach dropped. He was going to turn Sloane into a *bomb*.

"Her blood is the binding agent," I murmured. "The sacrifice is a smoke screen for his own spell. He's going to let them kill her for his own revenge."

"They won't get their power," Rick said, "and they won't be a problem anymore. Marini will be the greatest alpha the Fortitude Wolves has ever had."

Gasket shoved Rick back against the wall, and before he could move another inch, the wolf brought his fist down on his temple. The kid's eyes rolled, and he crumpled to the ground in a heap.

I cursed and began to pace. A binding spell? The bloodlines...

"Chaser." Gasket grabbed my arm to stop me. "You're losing it. *Keep your head on*."

"You don't get it," I rasped. "King is known to have sired all the vampires under the Hollow Men banner. It's how he controls them. If Marini links the bloodline, then all he has to do is kill one vampire and they're all dead. *Every single one...*"

Gasket's expression faded. "Chaser... Who turned you?"

I met his gaze, my heart twisting. "*Who do you think?*"

This time, it was the old wolf who began to pace, his brow furrowed deeper than I'd ever seen it.

"Marini has a talisman," I went on. "It's the thing that binds me to the pack—the tattoo is just an anchor. If I try anything, he'll use it against me. He'll use it to make me kill you. That thing… It's made from me, Gasket. The spell on it… It's unbreakable. While Marini has it, I'm screwed."

The old wolf's frown deepened.

I fisted my hands into my hair. "If I'd known, I would've let her go. *I would've let her go.*"

"You didn't know," Gasket said, watching my meltdown with a raised eyebrow. "You were only following orders. Hell, even I didn't know."

"Something's gotta be done. Sloane's timeline… There isn't going to be enough time to pull it off."

"Marini's becoming more and more erratic. I don't know what you've got going on, but you're right. This isn't the time to play the long game."

"Do you think you'd have the support?" I knew Sloane wanted to challenge for alpha but with our shortened timeline, Gasket could have the following we needed.

"Don't know," the wolf replied. "I'm well-liked, but that doesn't always translate."

I grunted. We had to work fast, then.

"What are we going to do about him?" I nodded at Rick's comatose body. "He's going to rat us out. No questions. We can't afford any leaks."

"I'll take him for a ride," Gasket replied. "A long one."

I nodded, glad I wasn't the one taking another body out to the bush or planting one in the remains of a car bomb.

"Marini will ask questions," I warned.

"And I'll have a story for him."

I narrowed my eyes. "You've done this before, haven't you?"

"More times than I care to remember." That was something else we had in common.

I was so done with this whole night. Turning, I took a step towards the stairs, but Gasket grabbed my arm and wrenched me back.

"Don't tell her," he said. "Don't tell her about Marini's plan."

I narrowed my eyes and pulled my arm away.

"She's not ready, Chaser. She's not supposed to be part of this world."

"I think you underestimate her capabilities," I drawled. "You've seen her break Harley's nose and change a few tires. That's not everything she is. Sloane is..." I didn't know the right word to describe the power in her. Holding it together was one thing, but sacrificing her freedom, knowing what fate might've awaited her, to fight back? It was something special. Even I hadn't been able to do that.

"She's not ready," Gasket repeated more forcibly.

It wasn't the ending to the night I had planned on

and not the way I wanted to see Sloane again, but around here, I couldn't choose my fate. It was all up to the roll of the dice.

"It's not about being ready," I said, walking away from him. "No one is ever ready to fight for their lives."

CHAPTER 16
SLOANE

The next morning, the compound was terrifyingly silent.

I must've drifted off in the early hours, but it wasn't a restful kind of sleep. It was the kind full of dreams that made little sense and left my head fuzzy and my eyes clogged with grit.

When I opened my eyes fully, I realised I wasn't alone, after all.

Chaser was sitting on the floor, thumbing through a motorcycle magazine. The light dappled across his legs—black jeans that were torn across both knees—and the tight muscle tank he wore clung to his chest just so. His hair was overgrown and hung over his forehead, much like the five o'clock shadow on his jaw that was inching towards beard territory. I never knew vampires could still grow facial hair, considering they were dead and all. *I wonder how that works...*

Realising I'd never had a chance to stare at him like this, I remained still. He looked tough, dangerous, and *handsome*. I couldn't imagine what he would've looked like in the 1800s, not even in one of those vintage daguerreotype photographs.

"I know you're awake," the vampire said, turning a page and tilting his head to check out a photograph.

"Where's Gasket?"

He glanced at me, cocking an eyebrow. "That's what's on your mind?"

"After last night...yeah, it is."

"Dealing," was Chaser's only reply.

He was doing that thing again. The thing where he told me with the tone of his voice that he didn't want to explain and I better not nag him about it, either.

"What did I do to deserve the pleasure of your company?" I rolled onto my back, thoroughly annoyed. I was the one who'd been attacked, and the garage had been bombed—probably because of my presence— but it didn't seem like a priority to tell me what was going on. I was dying to know how Marini had reacted.

"I've been ordered to keep an eye on you," Chaser said with a half-smile.

"Good."

"Yes and no."

"Do you have to always burst my bubble?" I grumbled, burying back into the sheets.

"Your father already suspects I've got a soft spot for you. This is just another of his tests."

"Just like the full moon."

Chaser raised an eyebrow.

"We haven't had a chance to talk," I told him. "I didn't expect it to affect me, being what I am."

"But it did?"

"Yeah…" I sighed, remembering the searing call of the wolf within me. "But I handled it."

"Another test," he murmured, his gaze studying me with a sharpness that tugged at my heart. "They seem never-ending."

"Typical…" I bit my bottom lip. "I'd really like to—"

"*Sloane.*"

I laughed, more out of frustration than triggered by any kind of joy. Nothing had gone to plan from the moment we'd met. Everything from matters of the heart to knowing which enemy to fight first. Even when I saw Chaser as the enemy, it hadn't gone right. It would be a comedy if the stakes weren't so high.

"What did Marini say?" I asked, rubbing my eyes. By now, my makeup was half up my face, and my eye shadow had probably migrated to make me look like a panda.

"He wasn't happy."

"You're not convincing me."

"This isn't working."

I knew he was talking about my convoluted plan to challenge for alpha. He'd said my father already suspected our relationship, which meant he wasn't buying a single word I've said since we arrived. We'd have to make a bold move soon, but not straight away. The attack on the compound had bought us some time.

"Where's Harley?"

Chaser shrugged. "Dead."

"*Chaser.*"

"He got blown to bits by a car bomb packed full of wolfsbane."

I bet he did. I narrowed my eyes and sat up. Something was going on, but the likelihood of him telling me was zero. I knew Chaser and Gasket were only trying to protect me, but I was feeling useless. All this was because of me, and I felt responsible.

"Sam?"

Chaser shrugged again.

"You just left her?" I exclaimed, sitting up. "You just left her alone with no idea?"

"My priority is you," he said, staring at me blankly. "You and this plan you've cooked up. *Our* revenge. *Our* future. *Our freedom.*"

Once, it would've made me jump for joy hearing him say that, but not now. Sam was vulnerable, broken, and completely open to... To what? Nothing good, that's for sure.

"I can't believe you," I said, kicking my feet onto the floor. Picking up my boots, I dragged them on. "You know how Harley treated her, but at least his claim shielded her from the pack. Now she's alone and without protection. You know what some of these wolves are like. She's *human*, Chaser."

He put down the magazine and pushed to his feet. "I heard she didn't want your help."

For so long it'd been just him, and now here I was with my big ideas wanting to save everyone, despite the promises I'd made. Maybe I was giving him whiplash.

"She didn't want my help then, but I haven't given up on her." I glared at him and stood. "Get out of my way." He placed his hands on my shoulders and I pushed against him. "*I mean it*."

"Wait." Lowering his head, his nose brushed against mine.

He kissed me, his mouth pressing against mine. I melted, opening my lips and allowing his tongue to sweep along mine. Fingers moved from my face into my hair, tightening around my messy locks. My knees weakened, and I almost fell back onto the bed, but he pulled back.

"Go," Chaser said, his lips brushing against mine. "I've got your back."

"Chaser..." I hesitated. I had a feeling this story was changing him more than it was me.

"I didn't want to be in this life," he said. "I've seen her... She doesn't want it, either."

"How do you know?"

He shrugged. "Don't push her."

I nodded. I knew all about that.

Moving towards the door, I wrapped my hand on

the handle and paused. "What else is going on Chaser?"

"Plenty."

"You're not going to tell me, are you?" He said nothing and I sighed. "I hate when you do that, FYI."

"All you have to worry about today is Sam," he told me. "Like I said... *I've got your back.*"

Looking him over once more, I opened the door. It was as good as I was going to get.

The compound was oddly quiet as I made my way from my room to Sam and Harley's.

Glancing up and down the hall, I knocked on the door. "Sam?"

Nothing moved. I pressed my ear against the door, but all I could hear was the *whoosh, whoosh* as my heart pumped blood through my body.

"Sam?" I pushed off the door and knocked again. "It's Sloane. If you're in there, please open the door. I'm alone."

The door opened a crack, and Sam's blue eye peered at me through the gap. A chain rattled, preventing the door from opening any farther.

"What?" she murmured, her voice husky. Her eyes were red and puffy and her cheeks all splotchy—proof of her tears shed for Harley.

I placed my palm against the wall and leaned in close. "You know what happened?"

She nodded.

"Can I come in?"

"I..." She sniffed.

"Please, Sam."

Her gaze lowered to the floor, but she didn't shut me out. Not yet, anyway. Then she closed the door in my face. For a moment I was stunned, but then the chain rattled and the door opened again.

I slipped through the gap and turned as Sam locked us inside, putting the chain back in place.

The room was decorated to Harley's taste with framed photos of motorcycles and sports teams on the walls. It also reeked of cigarettes and stale beer, though Sam had done her best to tidy the area. The bed was made with the sheets all tucked in with five-star hotel crispness, the table was free of rubbish, and the floor was spotless. I would bet my life the bathroom sparkled like a teenage vampire in direct sunlight.

"Nice place," I said, narrowing my eyes at a poster of a naked woman draped over a Harley Davidson motorcycle.

"I'm worried about you," I said. "Harley—"

"Don't say it, Sloane." Sam shook her head and bit her nails. The poor woman looked like she was a hair's breadth away from curling up in the corner and rocking back and forth.

"Has anyone hurt you?"

She stopped her nervous chewing and shook her head.

"But someone came?" I prodded.

"Yeah. Rocket."

I curled my lip in distaste. Rocket was bad news. It wasn't a secret he loathed me and knowing what kind of guy he was didn't make it any easier to swallow. I could only imagine what he'd said to Sam.

"I... I..." she sobbed and turned her back to me, hiding her tears behind a curtain of tangled blonde hair. "You must think I'm pathetic."

"No, I don't," I said, stepping around her. "Not at all."

"It's not meant to be like this. I know it isn't. But... I always thought he'd change. If he got what he wanted, he'd be happier, and things would've been like they're supposed to. Harley wasn't always like that." She glanced up at me, completely lost. "Fortitude did this to him."

I didn't know what to say to make it better. Words were nothing but a temporary band-aid. Hell, I didn't know if there was a solution.

"I'm sorry," I said. "I saw him hit you, and... I couldn't let him hurt you, Sam."

"It was *our business*."

I bit my bottom lip and glanced at the ceiling. What was I supposed to say to a woman who'd suffered at the hands of a maniac? A man whose death Chaser and Gasket had covered up to protect me. What was the right thing to do in this kind of situation? I wasn't a therapist or an expert. All I'd ever done was run away, read a couple of political science books, and wrote a few essays that came back with miserable grades.

There was one thing I *did* know. Sam was vulnerable. Rocket had already been here harassing her, looking to take advantage. I could help her with that.

"You have to think about yourself now, Sam," I said. "Harley's gone, but you're still here. You have to do what's right for *you*. For your life."

"If they…" she sobbed and wiped at her puffy eyes. "What'll happen to me?"

"I'll look out for you," I reassured her.

"I don't need your pity."

"*It's not pity.*"

Sam sniffed and sat on the couch, rubbing her eyes as she crumbled against the pillows.

"It would've happened eventually," she murmured. "With or without your help. I just…"

"You had hope," I said, sitting beside her. "That's not a bad thing."

"Yeah, it is. I love him… I… I mean, I *loved* him." She buried her face in her hands and sobbed. "I don't know what I feel anymore."

I rubbed soothing circles on her back, knowing I was doing a terrible job of making things better for her.

"This. Harley and I…" She choked back a sob. "It

was hopeless long before you showed up, but I don't know what to do without him. I have nowhere else to go."

"We'll figure something out," I said. "*I promise.*"

She looked at me with such hope in her eyes, I almost broke apart. I hoped it was a promise I could keep. God knew I wasn't doing a great job of keeping the one I'd made to Chaser.

CHAPTER 17
SLOANE

The already sweltering temperatures soared even more the next day.

Venturing through the compound, I heard rumblings about the explosion, the dead wolves...and none of it was good. I almost turned back, knowing there would be those who blamed me for the attack, and with four bodies lined up, a target was growing on my back. Orders from the alpha would mean nothing if tensions broke.

The Hollow Men had sent a message by sending that car bomb into the compound. It couldn't be more clear or punctuated if they tried.

My next thought was to go check on Sam, but up ahead, there was a lot of noise coming from the common room. The entire compound was in an uproar over what Marini would do next. The pack wanted *blood.*

"Hey."

I turned at the sound of DeLuca's voice. He was one of the wolves who I hadn't gotten to know well. He worked on and off in the garage and disappeared on 'pack business' more often than he was around to do an oil change. I remembered him carrying off Chaser the night we'd arrived, but other than that, he was a stoic shadow on the sidelines.

When it came to loyalties, DeLuca's were hard to pinpoint.

"You shouldn't be wandering around," he added.

I narrowed my eyes as a bead of sweat trickled down my spine. "There's a lot of things I shouldn't be doing, but I do them anyway."

DeLuca breathed deeply, his gaze sharp as he took me in. "You're helping Sam?"

His question surprised me, though I wasn't going to answer. It wasn't his business.

"She's well-liked around here, but that won't stop them."

I sneered, my expression daring him to try.

"A brother goes down and what was his becomes scraps for who's left," he went on. "The guys are already talking. It's the way of the wolf."

I wanted to break his nose, like I'd broken Harley's, but something in his tone squashed down my rage.

"What do you get out of telling me?" I asked, facing him head-on.

DeLuca smirked, his Italian-ness really starting to

bug me. Tall, dark, and handsome without the accent. He wasn't all *la dolce vita*, but I was sure he thought he was all that and then some with the ladies. If he had his eye on making Sam his new plaything, he would have to go through me first.

"I smell it now," he said.

"Smell what?"

"The vampire's wearing off, Sloane," he warned. "What are your intentions?"

I narrowed my eyes.

"Things are about to get ugly around here," he went on. "*Real ugly.*"

"My intentions," I said, taking a step towards him, "are simple. I'm not for sale. The pack is not for sale. And my blood is definitely *not for sale.*"

DeLuca smirked and nodded once. His gaze moved towards the common room. "Careful, *little wolf*," he murmured. "For all our sake's."

He walked away, leaving me standing in the middle of the hall, and disappeared around the corner.

I tightened my hands into fists, my inner wolf stirring. Something had shifted between DeLuca and I...an understanding of sorts. Was this how it felt like to be part of a pack?

Voices rose again behind me, and I turned and made my way into the common room. Heads swivelled towards me, and not all of them wore friendly expressions.

Spike, Ratchet, Stewie, and Hopper congregated around the pool table, talking among themselves. Gasket was leaning against the wall, watching me with a raised eyebrow. Ram, Watts, and Rhodes looked like they would rather be in the garage. Finally, Rocket and his gang of thugs were ready to crack some skulls. The smell of blood was in the air, and Rick was mysteriously absent.

Shondra, Emily, Raquel, Kelly, and Sierra were sitting in a circle, talking low. When they'd realised I'd appeared, they glanced up at me. Shondra glared the hardest, and I felt an overwhelming urge to punch her square in the nose.

"Sloane," she purred. "How are you, hon?"

I didn't like it when they called me pet names like babe, baby girl, and especially hon. It made my eye all twitchy with rage.

Before I could answer, there was a lull, and everyone turned towards the door. Sam stood just inside the common room, her eyes red and puffy. She was dressed in a plain black top and denim skirt, and her hair was combed and done up in a ponytail. If it were any other day, she would look normal, but it was far from it.

"Hey, babe," Raquel cooed. "Come sit here." She patted the couch beside her.

Sam gave me a tentative glance, then shuffled across the room and sat with the other women. They proceeded to fawn over her with thin reassurances and fake compliments. Exchanging a look with Gasket, he shrugged. Women weren't his thing.

I really wished Sam had stayed in her room

Chaser was nowhere to be seen and my heart sank. *Would Marini make him—*

Gasket appeared next to me and dragged me back against the wall. "I know everything, Sloane. It's time to stop pretending."

"Then tell me something true, Gasket," I challenged.

"This game is moving faster than you realise."

"Don't patronise me," I snapped.

"Marini knows about you, Sloane. He threatened Chaser with the talisman binding him to the pack and I hate to say it, but that thing is unbreakable. While Marini holds it, Chaser is trapped."

I froze, my heart stuttering in my chest. I asked him to come here. *I asked him.*

"Do you think he'd use it against us?" I hadn't seen hide nor hair of the thing that bound Chaser, but Marini had revealed it to send a message. While the alpha held it, Chaser was under his *full* control. "If he knows, then why hasn't he used it to take us out?"

Gasket shrugged, which didn't instill much faith in the matter. "Chaser knows what he's doing. We've got a chance. It ain't much of one, but we've got to take it."

"Why do I get the feeling you're not telling me all of it?"

"The less of us who know everything, the better.

Knowing too much is a one-way ticket to getting us all six feet under, girl."

I wanted to ask him 'what now,' but I clamped my mouth shut. I was supposed to already know—being the mastermind and all—and I didn't want to admit that Gasket was right. I was in over my head.

"This is going to end badly," I said, throwing a look at Sam. "You said you'd help me."

"I can't make any promises. You know that. I can't do anything that could out me with your father. My leverage inside Fortitude might be the only thing that saves you."

I opened my mouth to counter, but something felt...off. "Do you feel that?"

Gasket tensed. "What you're feeling there...that's the pack tearing apart. The attack went down just like the Hollow Men had planned."

"But if the pack is at war with one another—" Gasket threw me a sharp look and I clamped my mouth shut.

"None of this would've happened if Marini had left her to rot," a wolf barked.

"It has nothing to do with Sloane," Ratchet shouted. "The vampires would've attacked anyway. Trouble's been brewing for *months*."

"That's bullshit," someone yelled.

Gasket edged in front of me as wolves began shoving each other.

"Four pack members are dead," Rocket bellowed.

"Four wolves were dumped into shallow graves last night because of *her*!"

Stewie shoved Rocket, sending him stumbling back into Spike. "You'd defy the alpha's orders?"

"Marini's not going to do anything about it!" Rocket seethed. "Our packmates died for nothing! I want blood, don't you?" He looked around the room, but Gasket's bulk hid me from his gaze. "*Don't you?*"

The room erupted, but not in the way I was expecting. Fists began to fly, and I snapped into action.

Pushing Gasket aside, I strode across the room, grabbed Sam's wrist, and hauled her to her feet. I dragged her from the common room, ignoring the eyes following us.

"*Sloane*," she cried, practically running after me. "What are you doing?"

"Shh," I hissed. "Hurry up."

I couldn't chance taking her back to her own rooms, so I went in the other direction, taking the long route back to my bedroom. We made it back with no one challenging us, though shouting and thumping echoed all around as I shoved her inside.

"Stay in here, and lock the door," I said. "Barricade it if you have to, but don't open it for anyone except Chaser or me. Got it?"

"Chaser?" She blinked, looking lost and on the verge of breaking down into hysterics.

There wasn't time to explain, so I practically shoehorned her into the room.

"Promise me, Sam."

Her bottom lip quivered. "I promise."

"Is there anything you want me to get from your room?" When she stared at me blankly, I snapped, "*Sam*."

"M-my m-mum's necklace," she said. "On the bedside table."

"Is that all?"

She nodded, tears falling from her eyes. She was terrified.

I grimaced and glanced down the hall. "I'll get you out of this. Hold tight."

I slammed the door shut and waited until I heard the lock click before I moved away.

First, I had to help Sam get the hell out of this cesspool, then I'd worry about myself. I'd promised her. *Several times.*

Gasket was still in the common room when I peered through the door. He was doing his best to pull wolves back into line before more heads rolled. By the looks of it, half were for murder and half were not. To my surprise, DeLuca was going head-to-head with Rocket, who was up in his personal space shouting insults.

Marini was nowhere to be found, the absence of the alpha giving the pack free reign to lose the plot. Gasket was doing what he could, but the only person who could end the tension was my father.

Diving headfirst into the madness, I clawed at

Gasket's arm, pulling him from the room and into a shadowy alcove.

"Sloane, what are you playing at? You're the reason the compound was attacked, and right now, you'll end up dead regardless of Marini's orders. Don't be a happy accident, girl. Get back to your room."

I wasn't interested in self-preservation right now. Not when I was the only one who had the power and the guts to save someone who needed freedom more than I did.

"I need your phone and Chaser. Now." I clicked my fingers and held out my palm.

"What for?"

I clicked my fingers again. "Hurry up, old man."

Gasket reached into his back pocket and pulled out his phone but hesitated. "What for?"

"I need to keep a promise."

CHAPTER 18
CHASER

Leaning against the side of the car, I let my head fall back and sighed.

I wished I'd brought some blood with me, or at least a bottle of hard spirits. The scent of violence was stuck up my nose, my throat had an annoying itch, and death was on my mind.

Behind me, the compound was lit up with a thousand artificial lights, but darkness clung to the alley. The sky was tinted orange by the city. Always orange. I decided I hated it. Being alone out in the middle of nowhere with Sloane had been a nightmare, but strangely, it had been the calmest I'd felt in a long time. Maybe it was her, or maybe it was the lack of Fortitude.

Movement drew my attention, and I straightened up, my palm settling on the gun shoved into the waistband of my jeans.

Sloane emerged out of the darkness, her hand firmly in Sam's grasp.

I didn't want to know how they got out of the compound with no one noticing, but I assumed Gasket had something to do with it.

"Okay?" she asked, her voice low.

I nodded. "Clear."

Sam glanced at me warily, her gaze falling to the gun. I knew what she thought of me—that I was a cold, hard killer who cared nothing for nobody. Everyone said the same thing, so I wasn't surprised by her hesitation. She was here because she had nowhere else to turn to.

Sam had brought nothing with her, just the clothes on her back.

"Here." Sloane took Sam's hand and set something into her palm.

"You got it?" Tears misted Sam's eyes as she inspected whatever Sloane had given her.

Sloane nodded. "I promised, didn't I?"

The two women embraced and I turned away, not entirely sure if I was irritated by their display of emotion or saddened by it. They would likely never see one another again.

"You'll like Yvette," Sloane said. "She's got a daughter. Bringing her up on her own. She's going to meet you at the border, give you a ride back west, and give you a place to stay for a while."

I opened the car door and raised an eyebrow.

Sloane waved me off. "Give us a second, would you?"

"We're out of time," I told her.

Sam nodded. "He's right. If you get caught—"

They hugged again, this time a little tighter.

"Thank you, Sloane. For everything." Sam wiped a tear and got into the car. Fiddling with the necklace in her palm, she reached behind her neck and put it on.

"Take care of her," Sloane said to me.

I smirked. "I got you here, didn't I?"

Sloane's lips curved, and she pressed her forehead against mine. "What about Marini?"

"He thinks I'm scouting out the Hollow Men," I told her. "He wants us to think he's planning some kind of retaliation."

Sloane glanced at the car, but Sam was already sitting inside and out of earshot. "Is he?"

I tensed, conflicted about telling her the truth. After a moment, I settled on, "Not the kind the pack wants."

Sloane pulled back and I knew she was onto me. Her gaze studied mine and her scent was full of the wolf I knew lived inside her. It was almost time.

"Gasket's waiting for me," she said after a moment.

"Go. I'll send word when I get back."

I rounded the hood and opened the driver's side door.

"Hey, Chaser?" Sloane's voice echoed down the narrow alley.

I glanced over my shoulder. Even the darkness made her look beautiful.

"Thank you."

I nodded and slid into the car.

"What's with you two?" Sam asked as I turned on the engine and coasted down the alley.

I grunted, not wanting to talk about it. Sloane had started off as cargo, just like Sam was now. Difference was, Sam would stay that way. Unless Marini realised where I was, who I was with, and where we were going. The Hollow Men didn't rate a mention...*yet*.

"You fell in love with her, didn't you?"

"You don't know anything about my life," I replied, keeping my eyes on the road.

"I suppose not."

Thankfully, she shut her mouth because I was not in the mood for a heart-to-heart. I was driving ten hours across the country for her—*for Sloane*—risking my life to get Sam out. I didn't need another big-mouthed woman telling me what I needed to do on another long drive through hell.

"She's not safe there," Sam said, breaking the silence I craved. "She'll never be safe."

"She knows that," I shot back. "We know that."

"If you care about her, you need to get her out of there."

"Sloane... She has unfinished business with her father." It was all I could say on the matter. Trying to explain my past, Sloane's, and our current plans for taking Fortitude to a woman who'd become a widow less than twelve hours ago was impossible.

"You can tell me, Chaser," she said. "I'm not going back there. I can't." She snorted and sank back in the seat. "Harley was the only person who kept me safe, and even then, he'd become a monster. I loved him once, but I was too afraid to leave. There was still a part of me that hoped the man I fell for was still in there. That Fortitude hadn't taken him away from me entirely, you know? I was afraid to let go."

I tensed, her words hitting home. *He'd become a monster.* I was the same. I was a vampire, which made me a monster by default, but through the talisman I'd become the Devil himself.

"Everyone else, they might've liked me in their own way, but they didn't stop him hurting me," she went on. "Not once. Sloane was the only person who stepped in, you know. I should've trusted her."

"You had no reason to trust anyone," I said. "Not with a track record like that."

"I only trust you and this Yvette woman because Sloane vouched."

I gritted my teeth. I hated deep and meaningful conversations. I wouldn't even entertain them with Sloane, let alone Sam.

"No one ever stuck up for me like that," Sam went on, babbling. "Stood up to Harley. I can't believe he's gone... Just... Dead."

"Sloane stood up for you for a reason," I said. "She risked her life for you."

"You risked yours for her, right? You got killed?"

"It's my job," I snapped.

"No one voluntarily gets killed," she declared. "Not even a vampire."

"*I do*." I was so over this conversation.

Sam's mouth fell open in shock. "She's got you by the short and curlies, hasn't she?"

I screwed up my face. "Huh?"

"Kelly will be devastated."

"Who the hell is Kelly?" I scowled and rolled my eyes.

"Stewie's woman."

"Bet he'd have a few things to say about that."

"What are you going to do?" she asked. "When you get back to Fortitude? I don't think Marini's got good intentions. I've always been scared of him."

"Smart girl," I drawled.

"So?" she prodded. "What are you going to do?"

Thinking about Marini's plan to sell Sloane off to the Hollow Men, I narrowed my eyes. We were on the highway now, travelling away from the lights of Melbourne. Soon, we would be able to see the stars again. The *real* ones.

I grunted, signalling I didn't want to talk about it because I didn't know what I was going to do.

Whatever happened, it was going to be a

bloodbath. Sam should be happy she got out now. *Extremely* happy.

"We've got a long way to go," I said, turning on the radio. "You should get some sleep."

Sam sighed and nestled into the seat, rubbing her eyes with the sleeve of her cardigan.

"She's so got your balls," she muttered.

It was a long way to the border.

A full night had passed, and the sun was showing its face by the time we parked in the lot of a McDonald's near the highway. I left Sam in the car stuffing her face with cheeseburgers and fries while I sat on the bonnet, watching the traffic come and go.

Apart from our insightful conversation about who had or did not have the possession of my short and curlies, the trip had been uneventful. Unlike the last time I drove across the country, no one had shot at us.

Sam... Well, after a while, things kind of got to her. She'd fallen asleep after a while but had cried and sniffed straight across Victoria. Couldn't blame her, but I had no words of comfort. Harley was dead—I'd snapped his neck and covered it up to save Sloane— and there was nothing I could do about that.

Besides, I wasn't Sloane. Sloane knew how to use her words. All I knew was how to pull the trigger. The life I led at Fortitude had erased the one I knew when I was with Loretta—a life full of tenderness, smiles, care, and sacrifice. How did I get those things back? If I lost Sloane to the Hollow Men or her father, did I want to care that much about her? Loretta's murder had destroyed me utterly and completely. Her death had turned me into a shell with no humanity.

I watched as a red Suzuki Swift turned into a spot across the car park and lifted my head.

I vaguely remembered Yvette from the pub where I'd found Sloane. A tiny blonde with pouty lips. That and how much Sloane cared about her. The fact Yvette had just upped and left her kid to drive across the country to take in a woman she didn't know scored more points in her favour. She was taking on a lot for no other reason than Sloane had asked.

The driver's side door opened and a little blonde woman climbed out. Turning, she spotted me sitting on the hood of the car and glanced around. Inside the McDonald's, there were tables full of travellers eating their way through chicken nuggets and sweet and sour dipping sauce, but the far edge of the car park was empty, save for a few long-haul trucks.

The woman wandered over, her hands shoved into the pockets of her denim jacket.

Yvette pouted and looked me over. "I can't believe Sloane trusted you."

I raised my eyebrows. "Is that right?"

"How is she?"

"Fighting."

"She was always good at that." Yvette craned her neck and gave Sam the once-over in the car behind me.

I slid off the bonnet and opened the passenger side door.

"Your ride is here," I said, tapping the roof. I narrowed my eyes, warning her to keep her mouth shut about all things supernatural.

Sam got out of the car with a sigh and sized Yvette up. Immediately, she combed her fingers through her knotty hair and wiped the back of her hand across her mouth.

I snorted, earning myself a glare from Sloane's BFF. I could see why she intimidated other women. She was pretty and all, but she wasn't Sloane.

"Hey, I'm Yvette," she said, smiling at Sam.

Sam glanced at me, and I nodded.

"We've got a long drive ahead of us," Yvette went on. "We can get to know one another in the car. Are you hungry? We can get something to go if you are."

"Chaser already got me something," Sam replied.

"Good. I'm glad his surly arse was thoughtful enough to feed you." Yvette turned her attention to me. "You look after Sloane, okay? I'm holding you responsible if anything happens, you got that?"

"Sure," I drawled, handing her an envelope.

"What's this?" She took it and peered inside at the wad of yellow fifty-dollar notes.

"*Money.*"

"No shit, Sherlock." Yvette rolled her eyes and pocketed the cash.

When she didn't leave, I asked, "Why are you still standing here?"

Yvette scowled at me and wrapped her arm around Sam's shoulder. "Is he always like that?" she asked as they walked off.

"Yep." Sam gave me one last look and mouthed the words *thank you*.

I waited until they were in the car and on the road before I turned away. The things people did for Sloane never failed to amaze me. Gasket, Yvette, *me*. But she deserved it, right? Look what she'd done for Sam, a woman she'd known for a little under a month. It was always something with her. Passionate, reckless, and completely selfless. Sloane had a definite sense of right and wrong.

Gasket was right about one thing. Fortitude wasn't for her. I wondered what would happen if she managed to take alpha.

Shaking my head, I got back into the car, backed out of the space, and turned back the way I'd come. Back to Melbourne, Fortitude, and an all-out war.

Back to Sloane.

As the lights of the McDonald's faded in the background, I thought about the things Sam had told me.

Maybe it was love, after all.

CHAPTER 19

SLOANE

I knew Chaser would be gone for a few days, but it alleviated none of my stress. The entire compound was on tenterhooks after the brawl in the common room and it was only by some miracle of Gasket's supernatural beta wolf prowess that things had finally calmed down.

The garage was alive with talk, not all of it pro-Fortitude, either. It was my chance to sow some seeds of dissent among the ranks, but I hesitated in the wake of what'd happened. I was a fool if I thought I could take the pack without someone dying in the process.

The morning after the chaos, I was helping clear some of the twisted remains of the garage under Gasket's supervision when I overheard talk about Sam. People were going to notice, especially those with malicious intentions.

"Kane was talking about taking her last night," Spike said.

"We would've stopped them," Ram said. "I know we do some messed-up things in the name of Fortitude, but there's just some things I can't tolerate."

"She's gone," Watts added. "She got out."

"She got out, or someone helped her."

Eyes turned towards me, and Gasket shot me a warning glare as I attempted to move a twisted engine jack, complete with wrecked engine, across the garage floor. *If I could just use my wolf strength...*

"Sloane, don't even think about it," the old wolf said.

"But—"

"You did your part," he murmured. "Your part in her story is over now."

"So I'm just supposed to mop the floor and not do anything?"

"No one hurt her," Gasket said with a scowl. "You put a stop to that, but if it becomes common knowledge..."

Yeah, I knew.

I glanced at the wolves across the garage who were still talking about Sam's disappearance and swallowed a pile of vomit. They were decent considering what they were—Ram, Watts, Rhodes, and co—but I couldn't vouch for the rest of the pack. They were the men I wanted to lead, not the violent, psychopathic followers my father had cultivated.

"Yeah, but it's just for now," I muttered. "Saving one woman doesn't fix the problem."

"Damn, we'll be here all day." Gasket snorted and nudged me aside.

"You need to work on your muscles, Sloane," Watts called out.

"Yeah, you got a set of weights?" I shot at him. "Give 'em here!"

"Focus on what you're doing," Gasket said, leaning over me so the other men couldn't hear what he was saying. "Your life is just as valuable, kid."

"I know."

"Doesn't seem like you believe it."

"*I believe it*," I hissed.

"We have to talk once Chaser gets back," he said. "The time for watching and waiting is over."

"Do you know something?" I straightened, the engine jack forgotten.

"I know enough."

There was a slight hesitation, but I didn't press it. *Yeah, we were going to have a talk when we were all together. A long, in-depth, very animated talk.*

Grabbing a rag, I wiped the grime off my hands.

"I need to take a break," I said, nodding towards the compound. "Can I?"

"Yeah," Gasket drawled. "Just don't go breaking any more noses."

"Low blow, pops," I retorted, throwing the rag at his face. "*Low blow.*"

Flipping the bird over my shoulder, I was sent off with halfhearted laughter. They were still hurting after the Hollow Men had blown up four pack members and decimated their livelihoods.

A civil war was brewing, and Gasket wanted to stoke the fires. *We have to talk once Chaser gets back... Pfft.* I just had to look around to know only half the pack would up and denounce Marini.

It was still sweltering inside the compound. The whole place was as hot as a super volcano about to blow its top.

There was another Real Housewives of Fortitude luncheon happening on the couch in the common room. Shondra, Emily, Raquel, Kelly, and Sierra were gathered around an industrial-sized fan, their hair blowing behind them as it swung back and forth. They each had a tumbler of Coke—who knew what the alcohol to soft drink content was—and were wearing bikini tops and shorty shorts. They looked awfully depressed, and it wasn't a result of the humidity. *So they did care.*

"Hey, Sloane," Sierra called out when she spotted me.

I eyed them warily. "Hey..."

After their reaction to Sam's appearance yesterday, I wasn't sure I could trust them. They'd been almost patronising. Psychological warfare seemed to be their usual MO, and I wasn't down with it at all. I was a straight up in your face, tell it like it is kind of woman.

It was probably why I got along with men more. Hopefully, yesterday had shocked them out of their bad habit.

"You got a sec?" Shondra asked, beckoning me over.

Reluctantly, I ventured over to their little enclave. Kelly scooted over, letting me in on the edge of the fan's sphere of influence.

"How are you?" Emily asked. "After the other day, I mean."

I shrugged. "How am I supposed to feel about an all-out brawl over whether a pack of werewolves should kill me or not?"

Shondra snorted and flipped her hair over her shoulder.

"I didn't like Harley or the others," I went on, "but he didn't deserve what he got. The pack didn't deserve what the vampires did."

An awkward pause halted our conversation, the droning of the fan as it blew around the humid air filling the gap.

"Sam's gone," Raquel murmured after a moment. "Her room's empty, but all her stuff is still there."

"People are saying she ran," Sierra said, looking worried. "Where would she go? Everyone knew she had no family...none that wanted her, anyway. We thought we were it."

"After what happened to Harley, she would've been..." Kelly trailed off, looking rather pale.

"It would've broken her," Shondra said, her expression softening. "Sam couldn't stay here. She'd already been through enough." She glanced at me.

"She didn't have any family?" I asked, feeling nauseous. There was so much about Sam I'd never even known, yet... She had a chance now that she was out of Fortitude and on her way to Yvette. Yvette would help her get back on her feet, deal with Harley's death, and start anew.

"She only had Harley," Kelly explained. "She was kicked out of home at fifteen, and they moved in together. I think that's why Harley joined the pack. He couldn't support Sam or himself, let alone deal with his werewolf side, so he did what he though was best." She shrugged. "She hinted that things were different at the start. The pack changed him for the worse."

I nodded, studying the tattoo on my finger. Sam had said as much, but I hadn't realised how alone she was. *Not anymore,* I thought to myself. *Now she has Yvette. I know they'll be best of friends. She's so much like her.*

"I never liked you," Shondra declared out of nowhere.

"No shit." I rolled my eyes, making the other women giggle, albeit nervously.

"But what you did for Sam..." she went on, "that was really something."

"Who says I did anything?"

"We won't tell," Kelly said, keeping her voice

hushed. "Things are tough for women in this pack, even though we're wolves, too. No one looks out for us. Our men do, but not everyone around here is as good as Stewie and Hopper."

"And Ram," Emily said with a pout.

"If anything happened to them..." Shondra began.

"What we're trying to say is that we're on your page," Raquel finished for her friend.

"All of us," Sierra said.

Shondra held out her fist and smiled. "Anything happens, we got your back, girl."

I raised my eyebrows, not knowing how I did it. If I did anything at all.

Shondra clucked her tongue and wiggled her fist at me. "Bump it, girl."

Raising my fist, I bumped, causing the group to giggle like a pack of schoolgirls. Thinking about high school and the mean girl hierarchy I'd struggled with when I was a teenager, I smirked. There was no way these women would've been friends with me back then. I was so not a part of any crew—popular, outsider, or anything. I was a solo troublemaker. Now I was emerging as a strong ally.

Maybe there was something in this, after all. The game wasn't lost, not completely. I would still fight while there was a chance. For Chaser, for me, and for the women who were at the mercy of Fortitude.

"Oh, my God!" Sierra shrieked, causing my heart to spasm. "What have you done to your nails?"

"Bloody hell," Raquel said, slapping her on the shoulder. "Give me a heart attack why don't you?"

Sierra grabbed my hands and looked like she was about to cry. Full-on flooding rivers of salty, salty tears.

"What?" I asked with a shrug.

"They're ruined! Look at your cuticles! And there's glue and acrylic stuck to them. Did you chew them off?"

"I work in the garage," I said. "It's not the place for pretty fingernails."

"Oh, it's horrible." She clucked her tongue. "Stay right here. I've got to clean these up."

Letting me go, she rushed from the room. The moment she was gone, the women giggled.

"Wow," I drawled, not understanding why the state of my nails was so offensive.

"It's her art," Kelly told me.

"It makes her happy," Emily said. "Let her fuss."

"Your nails do look like shit," Shondra added. "A little acetone bath never hurt anyone."

"I've got a great moisturiser for after," Raquel said. "You can borrow it if you like."

I blinked, the fan sweeping in my direction. "Uh, okay?"

Shondra smiled and pulled me into Sierra's spot, which was a prime position in front of the cool breeze. "You're one of us now, girl. Part of the crew. *Get used to it.*"

Staring at my nails, my gaze fell on the healed

tattoo on my thumb. I wondered what my father would say about all this. Making friends, settling in. It all felt...temporary, and my heart sank like a rock. I had a bad feeling the past was about to repeat itself, friends or no friends.

Chaser...hurry back...

CHAPTER 20

SLOANE

Staring up at the mass of metal above me, I scowled.

This was not the kind of 'on my back' I wanted to be. Underneath a car, spanner in hand, learning about oil changes and axle shock absorption...whatever. The garage was still in a mess, but work still went on alongside the cleanup, and that meant the apprentice was on deck.

The thing I was lying on didn't exactly feel stable. Spike told me it was called a creeper, but that just made it sound weird, so I kept correcting him to *luge*. Luge sounded cooler.

Spike was beside me, pointing out what part did what, but I wasn't having the best time focusing on any of it. This was all temporary in the grand scheme of things. Pretending to learn about nuts and bolts while Chaser was out there with Sam was hard. What if the

Hollow Men reared their ugly heads? What if Marini found out what he was doing and used the talisman? Not knowing was driving me over the edge. I wanted to be there...to be with him and never let him out of my sight.

"I need a break," I declared, rolling out from underneath the car.

Spike followed me, grumbling all the way. "You're never gonna learn if you don't pay attention, Sloane."

I rolled my eyes. I want to tell him to shove his car up his backside, but before I could get the words out, a shadow appeared in the garage door.

Chaser.

My heart soared at the sight of him. His gaze met mine, and as soon as our eyes met, he glanced away without as much as a twitch.

"Sloane?"

"What?" I snapped, glaring at Spike.

He narrowed his eyes, then looked at Chaser. "You look at him like..."

"Like what?" I scowled.

"Like you want to eat him," he retorted with a grin.

I made a face. No wonder Gasket wanted to have a 'talk' when Chaser got back.

"What happened out there?" Spike went on. "When you and him..."

"Vampires were after me," I replied, not wanting to get into it. I had to sit here like a moron when all I wanted to do was run after Chaser and... *Man, I was so gone.* "Life and death shenanigans ensued."

"The Hollow Men." Spike nodded. "I hear there was a thing with a train and a bullet?"

"How...?" I frowned, not understanding how he knew.

"Word's spreading."

Across the garage, I spotted Gasket talking to Chaser. They exchanged a few words, then parted. Chaser went into the compound, and Gasket went back to work. I desperately wanted to ask about Sam, but now wasn't the time.

Word was spreading? I wondered if that meant dissent was rearing its ugly head. *The time for watching and waiting was over.*

"So?" Spike asked, nudging my shoulder. "You're into Chaser?"

My heart skipped a beat and I grasped his wrist, my strength biting into his flesh. His gaze met mine and I curled my lip.

"Settle down," he said. "Gasket thinks I'm Team Marini and I was, but..." He placed his free hand over mine. "Chaser's a lucky bastard."

"He took a bullet for me," I hissed. "I killed a vampire..." I glanced at the door, wanting nothing more than to go after him. "Did you see the way he just looked at me?"

"Chaser's always been like that," Spike replied. "That's what makes him so unpredictable...and scary."

He shook his head. "I can see why women are lining up, though. They seem to dig that whole dangerous vibe. He's a good-looking guy... I get it."

I raised my eyebrows, not liking the wistful way Spike gazed at me. *Great.* I was breaking hearts when all I wanted to do was break skulls, but if he was telling the truth about switching sides, then I could use a wolf like Spike.

Rolling my eyes, I shrank in on myself. "I guess I'm a woman, after all."

Laying back down on the creeper, I scooted underneath the car, signalling the conversation was over.

"Hey, Sloane?"

"No," I shot back, my voice muffled by the car over my head. "No, thank you."

<hr>

I sat on the roof of the Fortitude compound, studying the rise and fall of the Melbourne skyline, using my wolf vision to count windows on the skyscrapers.

When I got Chaser's message about a clandestine meeting up here, I could hardly contain myself. It wasn't exactly the alone time I'd been craving, since Gasket was meeting us, but it was a chance to be with him and not worry about burly werewolves watching our every move. Up here, we didn't have to pretend.

The rooftop door opened with a metallic squeal,

and my heart leaped into my throat. Seeing it was Chaser, I smiled.

He swept his hand through his hair as he walked towards me, his jaw covered in more stubble than usual. He had been out on the road nonstop for two days, but the scruffy look definitely suited him. It gave him a wild edge that made my ovaries go *boom*.

He sat beside me on the roof, leaning his back against the broken air-conditioning stack and kicked his legs out in front of him.

"Sam?" I asked, moving over so the entire length of my body pressed against his.

"She's safe," he said, combing his fingers through my hair.

Damn, that felt good. He'd never been so touchy-feely with me, and it was as comforting as it was alien. It was strange how things had changed so dramatically between us. It was as if Chaser had gone through something profound while we'd been apart. It was unlikely he would ever talk to me about it, but I felt it, nevertheless. I wondered if his humanity was finally settling into place.

"Good," I murmured, glad Sam was out of this place and had a future she could look forward to. "Yvette?"

"Her claws were out." He narrowed his eyes, giving away that he'd had a verbal spat with the feisty blonde.

I laughed and shook my head. "Then she's fine."

Taking his hand, I turned towards the skyline. The

weather had eased in the past day, the sweltering heat now a mere simmer...the calm before the storm.

"What now?" I asked, tightening my grip on Chaser's hand. "I don't have a good feeling. Whatever we do, someone's going to get hurt."

Chaser nodded.

We were all in the firing line, and he would be first. And what about me? I had a strange feeling of foreboding wash over me, and I shivered. This was all because of Marini. If he was out of the picture... If we assassinated him, it would put a swift end to all our problems. Wouldn't it?

I glanced at Chaser, hardly daring to put the option on the table. "If I asked... Would you?"

He narrowed his eyes. "I won't be your soldier. I've done that, and it hasn't worked out so well."

"So, that's a no then."

"We're equals, Sloane." He sighed, and I sensed another of his Yoda moments was coming. "I'm on your side, but murder doesn't fix everything. It would be easy to pull the trigger, but you have to live with that stain for the rest of your life. I have to live with the things I've done. I won't do them if there is no just cause."

"There *is* just cause," I argued.

"It's not that simple. Killing Marini is a temporary fix. The pack would still split in two and the talisman would be lost. We wouldn't be able to pick an alpha, the compound would be in utter chaos, and people would die."

I sighed and shook my head. "No matter what we do, there'll be war."

"I think it was inevitable," he murmured, "with or without you."

Maybe he was right. There were two clear factions within the pack—those who leaned towards their humanity and those who bought right into the animalistic predator of their curse. I knew which I belonged to.

"I can't challenge for alpha," I told him. "I don't have the following. I have a dozen wolves I can safely say would be on board. A dozen out of how many? Eighty? We're screwed. We can't take on my father with those numbers, let alone the Hollow Men."

"We're not entirely screwed," Chaser said. "There are options. None of them come with glory but being alive is more important."

"I like being alive," I agreed.

"So do I. For once."

Chaser tugged my hand, and I melted against him. Laying my head on his shoulder, I sighed.

"I just..." I trailed off, not sure he wanted to hear my sappy dreams for the future. A hard man like Chaser didn't do hearts and flowers. He did bullets and blood. He was a vampire after all.

"You just what?" he asked.

"It doesn't matter."

"Yeah, it does."

"I just…" I swallowed hard, glad he wasn't looking at my face. I was sure I was flushed red, and it had nothing to do with the temperature. "I just want to be with you. That's all."

"What happened to revenge?"

I shrugged.

"I don't blame you for wanting this to end," he said. "I wanted it to after Loretta died, but the talisman stopped me."

Lifting my head, I drew him towards me. "You tried to… You…"

"There's so much you don't know," he whispered. "How they look her. How I became a vampire. How I—" He broke off as his voice caught in his throat. "There's something I wasn't entirely honest about."

My expression faded.

"It wasn't an accident the Hollow Men recruited me," he murmured. "It was King all along. He was the one who turned me and set me loose on the world. That's the Hollow Men way." *Then he'd manipulated Chaser into joining his organisation.*

I couldn't even imagine what it was like for him, having zero guidance and not knowing how to control his bloodlust. I hadn't had much since I'd turned, but at least I'd had some. If I'd turned on my own—the thought of going through all that pain alone—I wouldn't have been able to handle it.

"It's still raw," I told him. "I understand why you didn't say anything."

"Raw and *humiliating*," he scoffed. "My whole afterlife has been one long manipulation...and I fell for it hook, line, and sinker."

I pressed my body against his, feeling the coolness of his vampire skin. "Don't be so hard on yourself."

"I thought I knew everything, Sloane, but after a hundred years I didn't even know how they enslaved me."

"What do you mean?"

"The tattoo isn't the only thing binding me to the pack," he revealed. "I believed it was, but it's only the thing that anchors me to a talisman."

"A talisman?"

He nodded. "A shard of bone taken from my arm, etched with runes and magic."

I tensed. "From your arm?"

"Marini revealed it to me to deliver a message." He lowered his gaze. "He will use it against me...and you if he has to. Sloane, I—" He grimaced and tightened his fists.

"If he orders you to kill, you won't be able to stop," I murmured.

"There's not a lot we can do about it," he said after a moment. "We have to keep moving forwards."

I stared at Chaser, studying his mannerisms. He'd changed so much from when I'd first met him in

Fremantle. It hadn't even been two months, but it was like night and day.

Was this what he was like before he got mixed up with the Hollow Men and Fortitude? Was this who he was when he was human? After the dust settled, I hoped I got the chance to know either way.

"You're right. We have to keep moving forwards. But if I can't take Fortitude, then it's best it's ended," I murmured. "It's not just about us anymore. There are men and women down there that I actually like, if you can believe it. I owe them. We can rebuild from the ashes...or Gasket can. The pack would be better under him and then he'd have the talisman. I'd feel better if he—"

The squealing sound of the rooftop door opening gave us pause. When Gasket emerged, our shoulders lost some of their tension.

He narrowed his eyes when he saw how close we were sitting, signalling his clear dislike of our relationship, but didn't offer any commentary.

"Marini's starting to wonder where Rick is," he said, sitting down.

"Wait... What about Rick?" I asked, glancing between the two men. "What did you do to him?"

"He went on a long ride," Gasket said wryly.

"We had to question him," Chaser explained. "And we couldn't allow him to squeal to Marini."

"Why?" I demanded.

Gasket glanced at Chaser.

"It's time to tell her the truth," the vampire said. "*All of it*. She deserves to know what Marini plans to do with her."

"What are you talking about?" I asked, my gaze flicking between the two men. "What plan?"

"There was talk of a deal," Gasket began.

"A deal?" My blood ran cold and a chill shuddered through my nerve endings. "*I knew it*. He's planning to sell me off to the vampires for their creepy blood sacrifice, isn't he?"

Gasket nodded. "That's not the half if it."

"There's *more?* Isn't a blood sacrifice enough?"

"He's got a witch to cast a spell on your bloodline, Sloane," Chaser explained. "Once King or any of the Hollow Men drink your blood, it will activate, linking every vampire he's ever turned as one. Then all it'll take is one dead vampire to destroy them all."

"I don't get it," I said. "Vampires aren't born, they're created. How can...?"

"Every member of the Hollow Men was turned by King," Chaser told me. "It's how he assures loyalty. The way he turns people...he makes it painful so when he ultimately takes it away, they're grateful. It creates a primal link, like a bond between pack and alpha."

I was beginning to understand why Loretta meant so much to him. Through her love, she'd broken the supernatural bond between him and King, but he was still linked through blood. Nothing could change that.

"But if Marini links the bloodline..." I turned to Chaser. "You'll die, too."

"I'm beginning to think you have no regard for your own life," he drawled. "You haven't asked once about your role in all of this."

"Oh, I understand plenty," I said. "I have to die in their creepy ritual for his plan to work."

Chaser grunted, his uncomfortableness at discussing his past showing. "Now it's your turn, old wolf."

I glanced at Gasket. "Bloody hell. I think I've already sat through enough bombshells for one day."

"This one, you have to hear, girl," the wolf grumbled. "You deserve to know."

"Out with it, then," I drawled, readying myself.

"I was the one who got you into foster care after your mother died," Gasket said. "Marini wanted you then, Sloane, but you were just a little girl. I couldn't let him take you."

I stared at him, dumbfounded.

"I kept him off your trail for as long as I could," he went on. "You deserved to have a normal life away from all of this." He coughed and for the first time, he looked nervous. "Your mother..."

"*What about my mother?*"

"They thought she was the wolf, but when they found out she was human, they—"

"*Don't*," I snapped, turning away. "Don't say it."

It'd been in the back of my mind this entire time,

but I hadn't wanted to face it. My mother had died because they thought she was the wolf who could turn at will...but she was human.

She'd died because of me.

"Sloane, it wasn't your fault," Gasket said, reading my expression.

"Of course, it was," I snapped. "She was murdered because of what I am."

"You can't control how you are born, Sloane," Chaser said, placing his hand on my thigh. "Only what you do with it."

I fell silent and pushed down my anger, letting my thoughts play over what Gasket had revealed.

That's why he was always around when I was little. Gasket cared for my mother and loved me like a daughter. If things had gone to plan, then I would never have known I was a werewolf. I'd know nothing about this world of blood and violence, and I wouldn't be the target of a blood sacrifice by a cult-like group of vampires.

Finally, I took his big hand in mine. "You loved her, didn't you?"

"It was a long time ago, kid." He sighed. "Let the past lie."

I let his hand go and turned towards the skyline. What a mess. Blood sacrifices, murder, conspiracies, talismans, magic spells...*in what world?* This one.

"Marini is as brilliant as he is psychotic," Chaser stated, voicing the truth that rested in my heart.

"And his blood runs in my veins," I drawled.

"You are not him, you hear?" Gasket said, laying a big hand on my knee. "You're more like your mother than him."

"He's still going to kill us all," I said, brushing away an image of my mum I'd rather forget. "Me in a ritual, Chaser in the aftermath, and you for betraying him. We have to do something."

Chaser grunted. "And we will."

"Who'll follow us?" I asked, fretting.

"The attack on the compound screwed us," Gasket replied. "You didn't drive that car into the garage, but it was because of you. A lot of wolves won't follow you because of that. Then there's Sam…"

"What about her?" I snarled.

"You took away what was rightfully theirs," Chaser replied. "She was Fortitude, too."

"You're defending them?" I practically shrieked.

"No," the vampire said. "I'm not defending them at all."

"But it comes into play," Gasket explained. "There are certain things people around here expect. They see you, and they see their rights taken away, no matter how messed up they are. Pack law isn't always the same as decent human behaviour, Sloane."

I knew what the first thing I'd change if I became alpha would be.

"We have a solution," Chaser said. "You already voiced it, Sloane."

I glanced at Gasket, the man I thought of as a surrogate father, the only family I had left. I had an extended family now, but that was besides the point. I looked at him long and hard, and I knew he was our best chance. This wasn't about me anymore; it was about us.

Gasket narrowed his eyes and nodded.

"It's time, old man," I said. "Their lives, my freedom, and Chaser's is in your hands."

He grunted and looked out over the city.

"This has to happen before Marini makes the deal or this would've all been for nothing," Chaser said.

"I hadn't exactly thought that far," I admitted. "I'd hoped to do things peacefully."

"It's an unpredictable situation," Chaser said.

"The minute I give the word, we'll round up those loyal to Marini," Gasket explained. "Once we've got him locked down, the others will fall back and surrender. Without an alpha, they'll scatter."

"What then? Are you just going to lock them up forever?" I asked.

"He'll force them to choose," Chaser replied. "Pledge allegiance to the new world order or..."

I felt sick, and I turned my face away before I retched. I would've had to do the same if I was still in charge of all this. It was yet another glaring indicator I wasn't cut out for leadership. I was Marini's daughter, but I didn't have the smarts to lead a pack of werewolves when I still didn't understand what it meant to be one myself.

"It's the way things are done," Gasket said. "And the only thing wolves will respond to."

"It's the best way to save lives," Chaser said. "We need to neutralise Marini as soon as possible."

"You've thought about this before," I drawled. "Haven't you?"

Gasket grunted. "Let's just say this isn't the first seed I've planted." *Well, this was new.*

"Typical."

"Wait for my signal," the old wolf said, climbing to his feet. "And be ready to move."

"Is that it? What are we supposed to do?" I asked, completely confused.

He smiled and strode across the roof, the door screeching as he opened it.

I looked at Chaser and he shrugged.

"You better get some sleep," he murmured, kissing my forehead. "I don't know when we'll get another chance."

I glanced towards the door where Gasket had disappeared.

"He knows what he's doing," Chaser said. "He'll have a plan."

"I hope so," I muttered. "I really hope so."

CHAPTER 21

SLOANE

I couldn't sleep that night.

I tossed and turned, my body sluggish yet wired to blow. It was a weird sensation, being on the edge of such a jagged cliff.

Fortitude went about business as usual, yet there was something in the air that didn't sit well with me. The garage was quieter than usual, the metallic clangs and the blaring rock music dulled as if I were swimming underwater. I knew Gasket was going to give the order soon, but not knowing was making me break out into hives.

My head swam with what-ifs and worst-case scenarios until the night after the meeting on the roof when there was a knock at my bedroom door.

Thump, thump, thump.

My heart hammered in my chest, and I sat up in

bed, swiping at the sweat beading on my forehead. I rubbed at the dampness under my boobs as well, cursing the heat and the nervousness-induced sweat.

"Sloane."

Chaser. Sliding out of bed, I stuffed my feet into my boots and unlocked the door. He slipped through the crack and enveloped me in his muscled arms, his vampiric coolness soothing.

"Is it time?" I asked, holding him tight.

He buried his nose in my hair and breathed deeply.

"Chaser?"

"They're already on the move," he replied. "They're moving the women to a secure location within the compound. Once they're safe, they will corral the men pledged to Marini, then take him."

I snorted, the notion of women being guarded like lost puppies not sitting well, but I knew it was the right thing to do. A lot of the women I'd made friends with weren't fighters, even though they were afflicted with the werewolf curse. They didn't even know how to fire a gun—which struck me as strange considering where they lived—but I suppose they relied heavily on their men for protection. Maybe, when this was all over, I could teach them. Give them some power of their own.

"I need a gun," I said, pulling away from him.

"Sloane, you can't go out there," Chaser said, holding me back. "Gasket's got this."

"I won't sit back and let everyone else do the dirty

work," I argued. "I wanted this, and I will be a part of it. I'm prepared to face Marini."

"I can't let you put yourself in danger. If he uses the talisman—"

"We aren't on the road anymore," I said, placing my palms on his chest. "You don't have to put yourself in front of every bullet. Not anymore."

"This isn't the same," he murmured. "This is more than that ever was. There's more to lose than ever."

"I was the catalyst, Chaser," I said. "Everything we've done has led to this moment. There are wolves out there I swore to protect, and I can't do that from in here. I have to see this through."

"Gasket and I will go after Marini," Chaser said. "Go with Hopper and protect the others."

I knew I was being kicked down a few rungs, but I'd take it. I wasn't sure I could face my father and point a gun at his face and not falter. That was an admission I had to face now or potentially suffer the consequences for in the heat of the moment. Chaser had taught me something on the road, after all.

"Where are they?"

"The upstairs kitchen."

I made to turn, but I hesitated. He had to know how important this was to me, right? I wanted my father to know I had a hand in his downfall. I wanted to see the look on his face when I walked into the room. When I saw him, I would finally know how he truly felt about me.

"I want to look him in the eye and…" I didn't know what I would say to him. All this time spent planning and plotting, and I hadn't thought about what I'd say to him.

Chaser grasped my waist and squeezed. "You'll get your chance."

I'd tell him to be safe, but Chaser didn't need good-luck charms. I edged around him and made for the door. *Game on.*

"Sloane?" I turned. "Take the back stairs, okay?"

I nodded, leaving Chaser to go his own way.

The way was clear as I powered up the stairs to the upper level. Ahead, light was trickling underneath the kitchen door, and I could hear murmuring coming from inside. Seemed everyone was already in residence.

I rapped my knuckles on the door, and it inched open, revealing Hopper. I didn't know him well, but ever since I'd helped Sam get out of Fortitude, he'd softened towards me. It also helped that I'd won over his girlfriend, Shondra. It was comforting to know not all wolves around here were into owning women.

"Come in," he said, opening the door so I could slide through.

"Sloane?" Shondra stood as I entered, looking on the verge of tears. "What's going on?"

I glanced at Hopper, who only shrugged. He'd told them nothing, so no wonder everyone looked shaken.

"Something big is going down," I said, glancing around the room.

"Like what?" It was a woman I'd never spoken to before but had seen around.

"Sloane, be real with us," Emily said.

"Hopper won't tell us anything," Shondra told me.

"He won't let us leave," Raquel complained.

"I can't even get Stewie on his cell," Kelly added. "Is it trouble with the vampires?"

The murmurings increased at the mention of the Hollow Men. Everyone was afraid of another bombing.

I sucked in a deep breath. How did you tell someone their whole life was about to change? If this went badly, who knew what was going to happen to them. Gasket's plan was simple, but there were so many things that could go wrong.

"The pack is undergoing a change in management," I said straight up. "You're in here so we can protect you from the fallout."

"*I knew it*," Sierra exclaimed.

"You did not," Shondra spat at her.

"It'll all be over soon," I reassured them.

"Who's leading?" Kelly asked, glancing at Hopper. "Who's taking down Marini? Chaser?"

Hopper narrowed his eyes, aware she had the hots for a man who wasn't his buddy Stewie.

"No," he drawled. "It's Gasket."

The room full of women visibly relaxed and talked among themselves. It seemed the old man's popularity extended to the female population *and* the big, bad, burly wolves.

Pop, pop, pop.

My head spun towards the door, and Hopper straightened, reaching for his gun. Was that an automatic weapon?

"Something's wrong," I said, listening to the gunfire.

"They weren't supposed to shoot," Hopper said.

"Do you think they were ambushed?"

"Maybe."

I strode towards the door and twisted the handle, but the wolf grasped my arm and wrenched me away.

"Do not go out there," he barked at me and realisation hit me square in the face.

Chaser had set me up. I wasn't here to protect anyone. I was here to *be* protected.

Lifting my leg, I was grateful for my flexibility. Using my werewolf strength, I smashed my heel down on Hopper's wrist and he yelped, dropping his gun. Breaking free, I dove for the firearm and snatched it up. Pointing it at his head, I curled my lip.

"No more games, Hopper," I drawled. "You can't make me stay in this room. I will shoot anyone who gets between me and Marini, *so help me God.*"

He grimaced and shook his wrist. "They were right about you. *Human my arse.*"

"Step aside," I said, the warning clear in my voice.

"Then go," he snarled. "I ain't gonna try to stop you again."

I reached for the door but was brought up short when Shondra called out my name.

I turned.

Her bottom lip quivered. "Be careful, okay?"

"I'll be fine," I said with a smile. "I'm tough, remember?"

I went back the way I'd come. Passing my room, I weaved through the compound, taking the long way to Marini's rooms.

I hadn't been there since the awful dinner I'd endured weeks ago. I'd hardly seen him at all, which was a glaring indicator as to his affection for his only offspring. The more I thought about it, the more I saw the signs. They were all there—the absence, the threats, the cold stares, the baiting... I should have known, but it was too late to do anything about it now.

Sounds of movement echoed along the concrete halls. Boots thumped overhead, voices called out somewhere in the distance, but I didn't see a single soul. It was unsettling.

A shiver ran down my spine as I stood outside the door to my father's room. If he was in there, I couldn't hesitate. There was no room for doubt.

I held up Hopper's gun and opened the door, tracking the barrel in front of me. I was ready to pull the trigger and cut down any bastard who got in my way, but it was pointless. The moment I stepped inside, I knew... My wolf senses told me exactly what I needed to know.

He wasn't here. Marini was gone.

I clicked the safety on Hopper's gun and shoved the firearm down the back of my jeans with a sigh. It would never be this simple. A girl could hope, but hope meant nothing when it came down to the wire.

Of course, he wasn't here.

Marini's revolver was sitting on the table. Picking it up, the mother-of-pearl shimmered on the butt as I tilted it to the side and checked the barrel—fully loaded. Had Marini left in a hurry? I doubted he would leave this treasure behind.

The revolver was heavy in my hand, but still, I slid it into the waistband of my jeans. It was getting full back there.

Opening the bedroom door, I stared into the lair of the monster and scowled. It stunk of him, gunpowder, sweat, and blood. Curling my nose, I backed away but not before a glint caught my eye. A ring was sitting on the bedside table, and as I approached, I instantly recognised it.

It was my mother's diamond engagement ring.

A memory surfaced of sitting in her lap and playing with it, twisting the gold band around and around her finger, watching the diamond sparkle. *Daddy gave that to me on the beach*, she'd said.

I took one last glance around the room before I left, the ring heavy in my palm. I didn't know what it meant that he'd kept her engagement ring, but it was mine now. The one and only thing I had left of hers.

It was mine, and I took it from him.

Leaving the bedroom behind, I put the ring in my pocket for safekeeping and went out into the hall. I had to find Chaser and Gasket and get this thing done. Lingering here was pointless.

Movement at the end of the hall pulled me to the right, and my breath caught.

Rocket.

The word enemy flashed through my mind. He hadn't seen me yet, but he just needed to turn a little to his left, and it was game over. There was nowhere to go except straight ahead, so I raised Hopper's gun and took a step forwards. Shoot or be shot at. At this range, the spoils went to the quickest draw.

I gasped as a hand wrapped around my waist and pulled me into a dark room. Instantly, my flight mode activated, and I lashed out, smashing the butt of my gun into my assailant's face.

"Bloody hell!" a male cursed. "Settle down, *amore mio*."

DeLuca.

I twisted, gaining enough room to bring my head forwards, then I reared backwards to smack him in the teeth with my skull. He grunted in pain and let me go. Turning, I saw the blood on his lips in the murky light and smirked.

"You're one of them," I snarled, aiming right between his slimy werewolf eyes. "Say your prayers."

"I'm Gasket's," he replied, holding his hands up. "And if you didn't notice, I just saved you from being gunned down by Rocket, *little wolf*."

"How do I know you're not lying?"

"Who do you think informed on Marini to Gasket?" he asked with a sneer. "*Santa Claus?*"

I narrowed my eyes. "He knew we were coming."

"It wasn't me, *amore mio*. It might've had something to do with Rick being strangely absent, don't you think?" He snorted. "Either way, you've got no options. We have to find Gasket and regroup."

His phone vibrated in his pocket, and he pulled it out.

"They got him," he said. "They're regrouping in the garage."

"They got Marini?" I should've been happy, but I was thoroughly annoyed I wasn't there to see him squirm. "Alive?"

"Hell if I know."

DeLuca opened the door and peered out into the hallway as a new round of gunfire erupted somewhere in the compound. It was farther away this time.

"I thought they got him?"

"Rocket is leading a group loyal to him," DeLuca

said. "That'll be them. Quick." He beckoned me to follow. "We've got to get back to the garage."

Fine by me. I wasn't staying in this hole a moment longer than I had to. I had overdue business with my father, and it was time to collect...*with interest.*

CHAPTER 22
CHASER

I met Gasket in the common room, where he was talking with Ram and Ratchet.

The wolves nodded sharply as I approached, then moved out into the compound to rendezvous with the others.

Gasket turned. "Is Sloane secure?"

I nodded. "I sent her to Hopper."

"Good," he said with a grunt.

I knew Sloane was going to rip me a new one when she saw me, but I had zero remorse. There was a target on her back, and unlike me, she couldn't resurrect. Dead was dead for her.

"You know the plan?"

"Of course, I know the plan," I drawled. "If he tries to use the talisman, you have to make sure—"

"I'll do what I have to," the old wolf interrupted. "Let's get on with it."

We went down the hall, keeping our eyes open for any ambushes. Gasket's werewolves had done their job keeping those still loyal to Marini away, so the way was clear. No one challenged us..

Outside the alpha's rooms, I listened at the door. My vampire ears didn't pick up on any noise and my brow furrowed.

He has to be aware, I thought. *So why hasn't he used the talisman yet?*

"It's quiet," I said to Gasket.

"Which means it's a trap."

"Of course, it's a trap," I muttered. "*Stand aside.*"

Gasket edged to the right as I kicked down the door. The wood splintered inwards with a loud *crack*, and I flew into the room.

Marini was sitting in his leather recliner, smirking as we barged in. I didn't have to do a sweep of the room to know he was alone. We'd expected a welcoming party...just not one so small.

"Welcome," the alpha said, rising. "*What took you so long?*"

"It's over Anthony," Gasket said, using Marini's first name. "Step down before this gets any messier." He raised his gun. "*Now.*"

Marini smirked and glanced at me. "I didn't think you'd be so stupid, Chaser."

"This isn't about me," I drawled. "It's about what you plan to do to *her*."

The alpha snorted. "Ah, I see Rick squealed.

Whatever. I still have plenty of wolves loyal to me. You see, while you've been playing your games, I've been playing my own. You don't have the numbers, Gasket. All you've done is start a war you have no hope of winning." He reached behind his back and Gasket's grip tightened around his gun. "You will never own Fortitude. After I told my most trusted wolves what I plan to do with Betty, they had no problem kneeling before their rightful alpha. And with this..." he took out the talisman and held it before him, "I can make sure you and your group of traitorous whelps never see another full moon."

"Drop it," Gasket warned, his finger on the trigger of his gun. "I'm warning you, Marini."

The alpha snarled and tightened his hand around the talisman. Pressure closed in around me and I gasped, falling to my knees.

"See how easy it is?" Marini said, looking at Gasket. "All I have to do is say the order, and he'll carry it out. A vampire bound to the pack by magic, unable to die, unable to say no. He's the ultimate weapon."

I pushed against the magic holding me down, but it was no use. I was bound.

"And still you turn around and use your own daughter," Gasket said. "You would kill her in your lust for revenge."

"*They murdered my wife!*" the alpha roared. "Or have you forgotten?"

"I forget *nothing*."

"Of course, you don't." Marini took a step forwards, the gun doing nothing to deter him. "You loved her, Gasket. Despite the will of your alpha, you loved her and conspired to keep my daughter from me."

"Sloane may be your daughter by blood, but you were never a father to that girl," Gasket snarled. "Not when you conspired to turn her into a *bomb*."

"You're not her father." Marini held up the talisman, his mouth curving into a malicious grin. "*I am*."

My eyes widened as I felt the alpha's will bear down on me. "*Gasket...*"

At the sound of my voice, the old wolf moved faster than I thought possible. He raised his gun and fired at me.

One shot.

Right in the head.

CHAPTER 23

SLOANE

The moment DeLuca and I reached the garage, my gaze swept over the assembled men.

"We've got them on the run," Ram said.

"The compound's clear?" Gasket asked.

Stewie nodded. "For now."

"Where is he?" I exclaimed.

Heads swivelled towards me as I whirled across the garage.

"Sloane," Spike started, but I wasn't listening. Reason could go screw itself.

"Gasket!" I roared, the revolver heavy in my hand. "Where's Marini? *Where's my father?*"

He grasped my shoulders and held me steady. I pressed into his palms, my hand tightening around the revolver.

"He's alive," Gasket said.

"I want—"

"Come here, kid."

He let me go and guided me through the assembled men to a car parked just outside.

Gasket opened the boot, revealing his prize. I stared down at my father, unable to feel a single thing. He was bound with his hands behind his back and ankles taped together. A blindfold covered his eyes, earplugs were stuffed in his ears—the super-industrial putty kind—and a strip of duct tape was stuck across his mouth. Total sensory deprivation.

He was conscious because his head flicked back and forth as if he sensed the light on his skin.

"I want to talk to him," I said.

"Not yet," Gasket said. "We've gotta get out of here first. The others will come back, and we can't defend the compound."

"How did you..."

"Someone tipped him off," he explained. "Knew we were coming for him, just didn't know when. If we'd waited any longer, he would've gone for you."

I shivered and rubbed my hands up and down my arms. Had it really come that close? Inches away from being sent to my death?

Gasket slammed the boot closed.

"Where's Chaser?" I asked, looking around. "I thought he went with you to get Marini?"

"He did," the old wolf replied. "Things got...complicated."

My heart twisted. "He used the talisman."

Gasket opened the back door of the car and gestured for me to look inside. Chaser lay across the backseat, his head at an odd angle, a single gunshot wound in his forehead.

I gasped and knelt beside the car. Reaching inside, I cradled Chaser's head and eased it into a better position. He wasn't all withered like he was when he'd taken a wooden bullet to the heart, so I had hope he would wake when his body had healed enough.

"I knew it," I heard Ratchet mutter. "Those two hooked up."

I glanced up at Gasket. "What happened?"

"Your father was about to order him to kill me. He knew it might happen, so he asked me to put him down if it came to it." He placed a big hand on my shoulder. "Don't worry, Sloane. He'll wake when he's ready. Spike dug out the bullet."

"What happened to the talisman?"

The old wolf patted his shirt pocket. "Safe and sound."

My gaze met his. "Can I have it?"

He shook his head. "It has to stay with me for now, girl."

I scowled and looked back at Chaser. I wasn't alpha, Gasket was. He was asserting his dominance already and it rubbed me the wrong way. Chaser's life was still bound to the pack, but at least it wasn't Marini who held the talisman, right?

Gasket sighed and turned to the assembled crew.

"We can't hope to hold the compound with our numbers. We need to let it go."

"We're split down the middle. Fifty-fifty," Rhodes stated.

"We've still got the women to think about," Stewie said. "They're tough, but I'm not about to put a gun in Kelly's hand if I can help it."

"We need a place to regroup," Gasket said. "Somewhere that's easily defendable with a road that we can watch from multiple angles."

"I know a place," DeLuca said. "Out of the way, but still close."

"What's it like?"

"A miner's cottage my old man passed down to me. In the bush, on a block of farmland away from the city. It's out in the open, but we'd see anyone coming long before they become a problem. Nothing much moves out there."

"Anyone else know about this place?" Gasket asked.

"No one knows about it, so we have a good chance of going undetected."

"It's a *cottage*," Spike said. "There's thirty of us, countin' the girls, *and* we've got Marini."

"There's room," DeLuca stated. "You'll see when we get there."

"Right," Gasket declared, taking charge. "DeLuca, mark this house on a map for us. We'll split into fives, take separate routes, and meet there in two hours. You've got five minutes to collect anything you want to take. That goes for the women upstairs. Merrick, Gage," he snapped his fingers, "do one last sweep of the compound and clear it out. We don't want to be leaving any presents for Rocket."

I hung back as the werewolves crowded around and synchronised their phones, watching the commotion unfold, though one eye was firmly stuck on the boot of the car next to me. I almost expected it to burst open like a screwed-up jack-in-the-box, but all was still.

"Do you need anything from your room?" Gasket asked, lingering beside me. "We won't be able to come back here for a while."

"No," I said, shaking my head. "It's just stuff." I had all I needed in my pocket.

He narrowed his eyes but didn't offer any commentary or reassurances. He knew I didn't need them.

"Then we'd better get with our road crew." He nodded towards the garage door.

"What about Chaser?"

"He'll wake when he's ready."

"I want to ride with him."

"Go with Hopper," Gasket ordered. "Too many high value targets in the one car is bad news."

"But—"

"Sloane." He placed his hands on my shoulders and pulled me towards him. "He'll be all right. You'll be all right. The hard part is over."

I narrowed my eyes, wanting nothing more to argue that he was wrong, but the longer we lingered, the more danger we were in. I nodded and allowed him to steer me towards Hopper.

"So," the younger wolf said as I sidled up beside him, "can I have my gun back now?"

CHAPTER 24

CHASER

When I came to, I was somewhere outside the city, laying on the backseat of a car that stank like wet dog.

I jerked upright, my vision hazy. "*Sloane.*"

Leather creaked as Gasket turned in the front passenger seat. Ratchet was driving, and he glanced at me in the rearview mirror.

"Sloane's with Hopper, Watts, Spike, and Shondra," Gasket told me. "She's fine."

"You shot me in the head," I grumbled, rubbing my forehead.

"You had it coming."

Ratchet chuckled but didn't add any commentary.

I righted myself in the backseat and peered out the window. The city was behind us, the orange glow muddying the horizon. "What happened?"

"Marini tried to make you kill me, so I shot you,

then knocked him out before he could pick his jaw up off the floor," the old wolf said. "King hit the bastard."

I grunted. He deserved it. "Where is everyone?"

"We couldn't hold the compound, so we're headed to a place DeLuca has out in the bush," Gasket explained. "Before we hit the highway, the group split off into fives. If anyone's following us, looking to take Marini back, they're gunna have a hard time figuring out who has him. We're low on numbers, but it's enough to get the job done."

"Where *is* Marini?"

The old wolf nodded towards the back. "In the boot, wrapped up like a little baby."

"How far out are we?"

Ratchet checked the GPS. "'Bout twenty minutes, I reckon."

I sank back and narrowed my eyes. My head throbbed as the last of the gunshot wound healed, but all I could think about was Sloane.

We wove through the outskirts of the city, watching for any tails, but we managed to escape detection, and by the time we'd finally merged onto the highway, we were clear. The sunrise was the only thing that chased us to DeLuca's secret hideout.

I pushed out of the car when we finally arrived, leaving Gasket and Ratchet in my dust. Sloane was already there, standing beside the rotting verandah of an old miner's cottage.

"Okay?" I asked, keeping my voice low as more motorcycles and cars rolled in behind us.

Her eyes were on the others, scanning for Gasket no doubt. The dawn was bright, the fire of it lighting her skin with a dusty orange glow.

"As long as you are."

It wasn't what I meant, but I'd take it. My gaze fell to her lips, and for the first time, I hesitated.

"I think they all know by now," she murmured. "You're all up in my personal space."

My lips curved and I caught her face in my hand. Our kiss was swift, but for now it was enough not to pretend anymore.

"Everyone's accounted for," Watts said, his voice breaking us apart. "We set the women up in the workshop for now. None of them wanted to stay in the main house."

"Why?" Ratchet asked. "It would be more comfortable for them."

"They don't want to be in the same place as Marini."

"Why not hold him in the workshop?" Rhodes asked.

"It's not secure," DeLuca said. He'd know. "There's a basement under the cottage. It's tighter than an arsehole down there."

Sloane snorted, and I leaned into her.

Gasket thumped his fist on the boot of the car. "Basement it is. Chaser, give us a hand."

I glanced at Sloane, and she nodded.

She watched us drag Marini out of the boot and dump him onto the ground. He groaned and squirmed, trying to fight his way free of his bonds, but even with his growing strength from the approaching full moon, it was useless. It was a pathetic sight, really.

"Follow me," DeLuca said, leading us into the house.

Gasket and I carried Marini between us. I had his feet, and Gasket had his arms hooked under his shoulders.

The basement had been carved out of the bedrock underneath the house. How they ever got the permits for that, I would never know—likely, there weren't any. Either way, it was secure, isolated, and the only place we could keep Marini locked up. If miracles existed and he got free, there weren't many places he could worm his way out of. Upstairs or through the access window. Beyond, there wasn't anywhere to go that wasn't arid and full of the men who'd defected to Gasket.

And Sloane. She was out there, with one hell of an attitude.

We threw Marini down on a chair in the middle of the dank basement. Gasket pulled out a roll of duct tape from his back pocket and taped him to the metal. A knife split the bonds on his ankles, and he was lashed to each leg of the chair before his arms were secured behind his body. His shoulders looked like they were about to be dislocated, the angle was so unnatural. It looked uncomfortable, which was fine with me.

Finally, Gasket ripped the gag out of Marini's mouth, tore away his blindfold, and unplugged his ears. It was past time to have a frank conversation. No more manipulation, no more betrayals. Just blood and truths.

"Dog," Marini said, narrowing his eyes. "After all we've been through, you stab me in the back."

"You would've killed us all," Gasket said, not missing a beat. "You were leading us down a dangerous path, Anthony. Your beef with King was only ever going to end one way."

"Under me, Fortitude would've amassed more power than you could've ever dreamed of."

Gasket shook his head. "You can't see past your own arrogance."

"I know how this is going to end," Marini drawled. "Or how you think it is going to end."

"It's not my decision," Gasket spat. "This is not a dictatorship."

Marini laughed, the sound sending chills down my spine. He was cold, calculated, and...*soulless.*

"You have no idea what it takes to be an alpha," he said. "It is a dictatorship, Gasket. It's hardwired into our very being. It's your curse...and my *blessing.*"

"Where's the witch?" Gasket asked, folding his

arms over his chest. "Has she cast the spell on the bloodline yet?"

Marini smiled up at him, his eyes cold and emotionless, but he remained silent. This would obviously be a drawn-out affair...and a painful one at that. I fought the ball of rage flaring inside me and clenched my fists.

"You'll talk," Gasket said. "Eventually." He turned his back on his onetime friend and made for the door. When I didn't follow, he paused. "Chaser."

I didn't move, my eyes glued to Marini's smug face.

"What did she ever do to you?" I asked, my only thoughts for Sloane.

Marini smirked and spat onto the floor. "She looks like her mother. I didn't need the reminder."

I raised my fist and hit him, the force of the blow jarring up my arm. Marini's head snapped to the side, and he laughed, his teeth red with blood.

"Betty's only good for one thing," he went on, his words hitting me right where it hurt. "She'll end up a sack of blood and guts like Loretta because of you."

I raised my fist again, expecting Gasket to stop me, but he stood back and let me smash Marini's face. My knuckles collided with the alpha's face, the collision doing nothing to sate my anger. After a few good hits, Gasket finally stepped in and dragged me away before I beat his head clean off his shoulders.

"You don't stand a chance," Marini gurgled as we

walked away. "You'll never be able to take King. *She's as good as dead.*"

We thundered up the stairs, and Gasket slammed the door closed, locking it behind him. It took all my strength not to turn around and finish the job, but at the thought of Sloane... I couldn't do it.

Shaking my hand, I stood on the porch, my anger still as hot as ever. Gasket followed me out, his expression just as tense.

"What are you going to do with him?" I asked, looking out over the open field. The sun had risen enough to coat the entire landscape in bright, bold light.

"Hell if I know."

I didn't have to look across the yard to know Sloane was staring at us. The deeper I fell into this thing with her, the more connected I felt to her whereabouts. Sloane was magnetic north—my inner compass would always point towards her. I hadn't felt like this since...

Since Loretta.

"You better talk to Sloane about it first," I said. "He is her father, despite the things he did to her. She deserves closure, no matter how messed up it's going to be."

"Yeah," the old wolf muttered, following my gaze. "I will."

"You going to give me the talisman?"

"I think I'll hold onto it for now."

I snorted. "Bastard."

I walked through the mass of tents, watching the comings and goings of the other werewolves with interest. They'd really put together a full-on campground in a matter of a couple of hours.

Ahead, there was a group of men busying themselves behind the house. I recognised Ratchet, Hopper, and Watts going back and forth to a car, taking out boxes and other supplies, and ferrying them over to the clearing where a large bough of a gumtree shadowed the whole scene.

They were setting up around a circle, taking their places on long logs and various camping chairs. In the centre was a pile of ash from a long cold campfire that would probably be lit by the time the sun went down. They had two cases of beer, various guns and weapons lying at their feet, and packets of chips and pretzels.

There was nowhere else to go out here, so I stepped over the log and sat. It was bordering on blistering, but there wasn't much that could be done about that right now. Hopefully, this place was only going to be forced on us for a few days.

"You and Sloane, huh?" Ratchet asked, handing me a beer.

"Where'd you get this from?" I asked, looking at the label.

"Bones brought it," he replied. "But you didn't answer my question. When did that happen?"

I shrugged. "Who knows? One second you're whatever, the next..."

Hopper laughed and popped the top off his beer. "Was the same with Shondra. One minute I was a lone wolf, then...*boom*."

"Good for you," Ratchet said, punching my arm. "Never thought you had a heart."

"Only someone like Sloane could catch him," Watts said, taking a bottle from the case and sitting on the end of the log.

I grunted and opened my beer, immediately necking it.

"It was you, wasn't it? Who got Sam out of the compound? You and Sloane."

I scowled, not liking how big Watts's mouth was getting. He talked too much about the wrong things.

"Rocket would've—"

"Shut your mouth," Ratchet said with a growl. "We know what Rocket would've done. She's gone. Good for her. She didn't deserve that."

"And Harley did?" Watts asked.

"It had nothing to do with Sloane," Hopper declared. "The vampires would've attacked sooner or later. And besides, we all saw what Harley was doing to Sam, and none of us did anything."

I tensed, knowing that none of the wolves— other than Gasket—knew it was me who had snapped Harley's neck. Maybe it was best it remained that way. There was enough going on without dropping another bomb on the fractured pack.

"What's going on with Marini?" Rhodes asked, changing the subject before fists came out. "Any news?"

"Don't know," I replied. "Gasket's still working him."

"But you went in there with him," Watts argued. "Are you his beta now or something?"

"No," I snapped. "I'm a vampire, not a wolf. Someone else deserves to be Gasket's second."

"Like who?" Hopper asked, scratching his beard.

"We've got bigger fish to fry," Ratchet replied. "That'll come later. Anyone who wants that will have to prove themselves in all this."

"Ol' *Rat Shit* here is right," Spike said, joining us. "A lot of stuff has to go down before we can get Fortitude back up. I'm just glad we got Marini out. I didn't like where he was taking the pack. A little blood now versus an ocean of it later. I know which was my pick."

"Me, too," Watts said, taking another sip of his beer.

"On that, we agree," Ratchet replied.

"What do you think, Chaser?"

It didn't matter what I thought. When this was over, I was entirely sure I was going leave the pack and never look back if that was what Sloane and I agreed on. Ultimately, it depended on what happened next. Gasket still held the talisman, the Hollow Men still had it out for Sloane, and half of Fortitude was still out there looking for blood of their own. The war was only getting started.

"It doesn't matter what I think," I said, voicing my thoughts. "I trust Gasket. I'll follow his lead." *For now.*

"Shit, if Chaser trusts Gasket, we should all be in one hundred percent," Spike declared.

"That's why we're here," Ratchet said, smacking him on the back of the head. "No one plays his part in a hostile takeover without all that."

Lifting my beer to my lips, I thought about Sloane. All in, *one hundred percent.*

CHAPTER 25
SLOANE

The sun out in the bush was just as blistering as it was in the city.

I sat on a rock, partly covered by the shade of a twisted, ancient gumtree. Dirt and dust clung to the toes of my boots, and I lazily drew a pair of smiley faces on each toe. My arms were pinking up, which didn't bode well—I hated sunburn.

I pushed up my sunglasses—the pair of five-dollar aviators I made Chaser buy for me out on the road. That day had been barely two months ago. *What a ride...*

The cottage DeLuca had brought us to was nothing like what I'd imagined on the way over here. Instead of a tiny, single-room shack with a rocking chair on the porch, it was almost a whole sprawling farm setup. There was a yard where all the motorcycles and cars fit, a shed with a workshop inside, the cottage had two bedrooms, an open kitchen, living and dining rooms, plumbed bathroom, the whole bit—*and* it was hooked up to rainwater tanks and a generator. Problem was, the water was in short supply after a long drought, but beggars couldn't be choosers.

There was even a rudimentary basement carved out of the bedrock underneath the main house. From my perch, I could see the access hole in the side of the foundation. It was a small rectangle set with glass, covered with a layer of grit. No seeing in...or out.

I knew my father sat down there, tied up, being questioned by Gasket. Chaser was there, too. I wanted to be there too, but my plans for leading the pack had been taken out of my hands a long time ago.

What was it about this life? Every day felt like a year. Dragging its heels to claw out maximum pain.

It was deathly quiet for a place that held half the population of the ragged remains of the Fortitude Wolves. All forty-eight. Twenty had descended last night, and ever since, other allies had been steadily arriving—those who'd been out on jobs, others who didn't live at the compound, those who had families to protect. Not all could be there for the initial strike. Gasket trusted them, and by extension, so did I.

They'd brought supplies, tents, and camping gear with them, and a miniature city had formed in the yard behind the cottage. No one wanted to stay in a house where Marini was being held, and I couldn't blame them. I sat apart from it all, not knowing how to be around people. I was the cause of this, after all—*the wolf who could turn at will.* I wondered how much they knew.

The front door of the cottage opened, and my heart leaped into my throat. Gasket appeared, his boots thumping on the verandah, and Chaser stepped out behind him. The old wolf leaned against the rail, looking as tired as I felt. Chaser stood tall, but he always did. Nothing cracked the surface with him.

They exchanged a few tense words—but it was too swift for my enhanced hearing to pick up—then went their separate ways. Chaser walked towards the tent city, but Gasket came towards me.

His boots crunched on the rocky ground, his eyes squinting in the bright sunshine. Marini must've told them something.

"Any room on that rock, girl?" Gasket asked, towering over me.

I slid over, and he sat, though we hardly fit on it at all. My right arse cheek was hanging off the edge, and the revolver I'd refused to relinquish pressed into the small of my back.

"You smell like crap," I said, delaying the inevitable.

"There was no remorse in him, kid," he said, ignoring my insult. "I'm sorry."

"It's not your fault I share DNA with a psychopath."

He grunted and rubbed his eyes with his big fist.

"Have you slept?"

He shook his head. "Have you?"

"Can't," I replied.

"That ain't good for your health."

"What's going to happen now?"

Gasket lowered his head, his gaze studying the dusty smiley faces I'd drawn on my boots.

"We have no choice," he said. "If you want to talk to him before... Chaser or I will go with you."

I rose to my feet and moved a few steps towards the nothingness of the bush. *Before they killed him?* My stomach rolled, even though I knew this was the inevitable outcome. He was still my father. He'd loved my mum once, didn't he? He had her engagement ring, so there had to be some feeling...right?

"Sloane?"

I raised my gaze towards the sky, finding the blue endless. Out there, where the sky became dark, was a universe larger than any of us. We were insignificant and pointless.

What was the point?

"Not today," I said. "Maybe tomorrow."

That night, I still hadn't managed to gather enough courage to return to camp. The moon was nearing its apex, casting a silver glow clear across the open field, and the wolf within thrashed at the edges of my psyche.

I'd only turned once, and I wasn't requited to again,

but I felt the draw of it all the same. The rest of the pack would have to turn in a few days, but where?

"Gasket said you'd walked off."

Turning, I saw Chaser looming out of the landscape, weaving between the scrappy undergrowth.

"I wanted to be alone."

"I know. Just wanted to make sure you weren't lost."

"Of course not. I can sniff my way back."

"*Of course.*" He sat beside me, pressing into my side. He just melted into me like it was the most natural thing in the world. We were two pieces of a puzzle slotting together.

"*Of course,*" I drawled, turning my face towards him. "I've got an amazing sense of direction without my werewolf superpowers."

"You're not worried about being out here in the dark?" he asked, lifting an eyebrow.

I snorted, thinking back to the night we'd been run off the road by two Hollow Men. I hadn't liked the way the wild landscape had made me feel, but now I craved it. The isolation was soothing, and now that Chaser was here, it was perfect.

"I can see why you like looking at the sky," I said. "I can barely count a handful, let alone them all."

"No one can count them all," Chaser said, glancing up. "There are stars out there whose light has never reached us at all. Maybe it never will."

"Do you regret it?" I asked.

"What?"

"Starting all this?"

"Why are you asking?" He was avoiding the question, and it made me bristle

"I think about it sometimes," I murmured. "If I'd escaped, or if you'd let me go."

"I don't believe in what-ifs," he stated. "After I was bound to the pack, I..." He sighed. "At first, I dwelled on them to the point it drove me to despair. You can't build a life on what *might've* happened."

"I imagine that's why you're so..." I trailed off, not wanting to be that person. The person who stuck the emotional knife in and twisted.

"Inhuman?" Chaser asked. "Was that the word you were going for?"

I grunted, turning my face so he couldn't see the regret pooling in my eyes. I shouldn't have said that. After everything he'd been forced to endure, turning away from his humanity was his only choice.

"We all deal with our shit in different ways," he went on. "This is mine."

"I didn't mean..."

His arm snaked around my back. "We are who we are, Sloane. People never change, not really. Not even vampirism or lycanthropy can change who we truly are. Views and motivations might, but our core always remains the same."

I took his words as a hopeful sign that underneath all his bland indifference was the man he was before his life had changed for the worse.

"You don't want to speak to your father?" he asked when I finally turned my gaze on him.

"Not today." I shook my head. "I don't even know what to say to him. I can already anticipate his answers, so it's like...why bother?"

Chaser tightened his embrace.

"Besides, we still have to worry about the other half of Fortitude...the renegades. Then there's still the Hollow Men," I added. "They still want me for their blood sacrifice."

"What do you want, Sloane?"

"Huh?" I thought we'd already worked that out. Freedom for all. The end.

"What happens after this?" Chaser asked. "If we get what we want, then what?"

Ah, the bit *after* the end. I shrugged. "I always thought Fortitude as we know it would be disbanded and rebuilt into a family. Continuing to run the pack as a glorified criminal organisation isn't right. Though, nothing has exactly turned out like I'd hoped." I turned my gaze on him. "What about you?"

"I don't know," he admitted. "I've been so fixated on revenge, I got lost in my rage. I saw nothing past that... not until I told you I'd leave it all behind."

My heart swelled, and I leaned my forehead against his. "You did, didn't you?"

"It's hard for me," he murmured. "Saying these things."

"I know."

"I've held onto her for so long..."

I didn't want to feel jealous of a dead woman, but I couldn't help it. He'd loved Loretta so much that they'd married, and in the aftermath of her passing, he'd given up everything to go after the bad guys. I wanted to inspire that much love and devotion in someone, but it wasn't something I could make happen. Love was fickle and only reared its head when it was good and ready.

Still, I wanted Chaser to love me like he'd loved Loretta.

"We're fighting for something better," I said. "Revenge isn't the right word anymore. I doubt it ever was."

"Then what is?"

I thought about it for a moment. We wanted to take over the pack—granted, that didn't work out—and unite against the threat of the Hollow Men. We both had our reasons, but maybe it was more about justice for the wrongs that had been committed against us. For Chaser, it was what'd happened to Loretta and his century of forced servitude. For me, it was what my father had planned to do to me, now and then. We'd both picked up a few more bullet points along the way to solidify our cause, but it all boiled down to the one thing.

"Justice," I whispered.

Chaser grunted, his opinion on the matter remaining a secret.

"See that star with the red tinge?" he asked after a moment. "That's Mars."

"Really?"

"And that's Venus on the horizon..." he trailed off, his body tensing as we saw the same anomaly.

"What's that light?" I asked, rising to my feet.

Chaser stood and grasped my arm, tugging me behind him. Something was wrong. I could feel it in my bones.

"Fire," he said. "The cottage is on fire."

CHAPTER 26

SLOANE

"Who do you think it is?" I asked, reaching for my gun.

"The other half of the sword," Chaser replied, rubbing his finger over the tattoo on my thumb.

He was right. It couldn't be anyone else.

"Do you think we have a mole?" I asked, feeling the weight of the revolver pressing into my back.

"Doesn't matter now."

Gunfire popped in the distance, and I broke out into a run with Chaser hot on my heels.

"*Sloane*," he exclaimed behind me. "*Stop*."

I'd cowered behind Chaser all those times on the road; I'd run from danger and did nothing to save myself. I was beginning to doubt I'd fought at all, but now I had the power and the guts to point and shoot. I wouldn't let anyone take away my justice.

Pulling the revolver out from the waistband of my

jeans, I hurtled towards the smoke and flames, driven by the shouting and gunshots. The wolves who'd followed us into this mess were fighting for their lives. Good men. Ratchet, Watts, Rhodes, Spike, Butcher, Hopper, Stewie...all of them.

A bullet flew past my head, the shot so close I felt air rush past my skin. Cursing, I ducked behind the closest car and pressed my back against the door. Chaser was beside me in a flash, looking like he was about to unleash Armageddon on anyone who came close.

"Do you see anyone?" I asked, holding the revolver at the ready.

He shook his head. "Smoke's blowing this way. Even I can't see through that."

Gasket appeared out of a plume of smoke, firing at a man brandishing a shotgun at his head. The man dropped, and the wolf slid behind the car we were using as cover.

"Gasket," I said, clutching his arm. It was red with blood, but it didn't seem to be his.

"They came out of nowhere," the old wolf said. "Someone tipped them off to our location."

"No shit," Chaser replied.

"They brought war on us," I stated. "Do unto others, or so they say."

"You don't want that stain on your soul, girl."

I eyed Gasket and shrugged. "Too late, old man."

"We're going to go around the back and cut them

off," Gasket went on, narrowing his eyes at me. "Surround them and force surrender."

"Then what?" Chaser asked with a scowl. "Lock them up in the basement and give them parole hearings?"

"We'll figure that out once they stop shooting."

"The only way this will end is by not stopping," Chaser growled. "Keep firing until the cowards run and the stupid die." He leaned over me and eyeballed Gasket. "All you have to do is say the word and I'll finish them off."

"I won't have this turn into a bloodbath, Chaser."

"They will kill everyone, Gasket," the vampire hissed. "*Everyone*."

My blood ran cold. It wasn't just men here. There were women as well. I doubted that mattered to the renegades. Women died just the same.

"Where are the women?" I asked. "Where's Shondra, Kelly, and the others?"

"Hopper and DeLuca got them out once the first shots were fired," Gasket replied. "They're out in the bush someplace. DeLuca knew where he was going."

A rain of bullets clipped the car we were taking cover behind, and I ducked my head. The sound was awful. *Thwack, thwack, thwack.*

"Who cares," I declared. "We've got to move before they blow the tank on this car."

Chaser curled his hand around my arm. "You're with me."

"Obviously."

Gasket nodded. "Go. I'll cover you." He leaned over the top of the car and fired.

Chaser and I ran, working our way around the edge of the cabin and through the tents.

Smoke and gunfire were everywhere, disorienting my movements. If it weren't for Chaser, I would already be lost in the chaos.

Deep breaths, Sloane. I breathed in, the air tinged with the rank taste of the firefight. I stepped over a body, then another—their wolf-eyes wide open and vacant, their bodies torn by bullets.

Chaser dragged me behind the workshop, and we peered around the corner, surveying the scene.

"Stay here," he said after a moment. "Take cover, and don't make a sound."

"You can't bench me," I complained, my entire body humming with adrenaline. "Not now."

"This is not up for debate. If anything happens to you..." He grasped my face.

Chaser's eyes were full of something I'd never seen in them before. Fear. He'd lost before, and he was afraid of losing again. First Loretta and now... *No.*

"That's not going to happen," I said, prying his hands away. "I'm a wolf, Chaser. I'm strong, maybe not vampire strong, but I've got more power than—"

"The moon is almost full," he interrupted. "*You don't.*"

"I'm not arguing with you while more wolves die."

Chaser let out a frustrated growl as I leaned around the corner of the workshop and scanned the yard. It was quieter around here, and I could see the only access to the basement where Marini was being held. The cottage was on fire, the flames spiralling towards the sky. The heat radiating off the building was increasing as the inferno took hold, eating its way towards the back.

There was no way of knowing if Marini was still down there or if he'd been freed before the fire was set. If he was trapped, the only way out was the window I was staring at.

"If my father tries to escape, we have to stop him."

"If he's still down there," Chaser replied, voicing my thoughts. He'd seemed to have resigned himself to the fact that I was going to fight no matter what. Once this was over, I was positive there was going to be a 'discussion' about the clear reemergence of my 'too stupid to live' attitude.

Leaning back around, I trained my gaze on the window, hesitating when a group of men rounded the opposite side of the cabin. There were four, and they all broke off as they searched the tents.

I saw Rocket advance with a shotgun in his hands and my blood boiled.

"You've only got six shots in there," Chaser murmured in my ear. "Don't let them go all at once."

"Shotguns are slow," I retorted. "Two shots, slow reload."

"Wrong. He's got five, with a minimum fifteen-second reload speed, not to mention he's high on bloodlust and strengthened by the approaching full moon."

The sound of breaking glass turned my head and smoke billowed out of the basement window. I clawed at Chaser's arm as a head emerged. *Marini*.

Before I could do anything, Chaser strode out from behind the workshop and raised his gun and fired. One, two, three. Bodies dropped. My heart stopped as Rocket turned and aimed the shotgun right at his chest, then he fired again. Four.

Holy shit.

Marini had wormed his way out of the window, his head turning from side to side. He saw Chaser looming through the mass of tents, saw his men lying dead on the ground, and scrambled to his feet. Then, he ran.

Chaser aimed but couldn't seem to get a clear shot. He tensed, his muscles coiling as he moved to pursue, but before he could take off, I made my move.

Pushing off the wall, I sprinted after Marini as he broke out into a run and disappeared into the bush.

"*Sloane!*" Chaser roared, but I wasn't listening. I only had eyes for Marini.

I sprinted through the darkness, dodging low-hanging branches and leaping over rocks, following the sound of my father's pounding footsteps as he ran in front of me. Behind us, the glow of the burning cottage faded and the sounds of the firefight dulled.

I could see his back as he flitted through the landscape, fleeing into the bush. He dashed to the side, doubling back towards the road and the renegades. I never missed a beat. My heart galloped in my chest, my lungs burning and my thighs aching with exertion. There was no way in hell I was letting him get away.

He twisted and leaped, throwing me off his tail for a split second. It was all it took. I skidded to a halt and held the revolver at the ready, the sound of my heart thumping in my ears and my laboured breathing loud in the nothingness.

I'd barely practiced with my new wolf abilities, but I tried now. My hearing sharpened and my wolf sight illuminated the darkness. I felt the power of the moon above and my bones began to ache.

I took a step forwards. He had to be lurking somewhere, hiding behind a bush like the coward he was.

There was no love left in me for him now. To be honest, I doubted there ever was. The love of an innocent child, perhaps, but not the kind he deserved. Gasket was a thousand times the man Anthony Marini was.

I took another step, the revolver shaking in my hands. What was I going to do when I caught him? Was I going to shoot him? Could I pull the trigger? I couldn't even face him down in that basement.

Marini leaped out of the darkness and swung his fist at me. At the last second, I realised he was clutching a large rock and ducked to the side. His fist *whooshed* past my head, causing him to swing and show his back to me. I slammed my elbow into the base of his spine with a cry, and he stumbled forwards.

Swinging, I raised the revolver and aimed it right at him.

"I will shoot you, so help me God," I snarled.

Marini righted himself and turned to face me, the rock still clutched in his hand. His silver hair shone in the moonlight, his body silhouetted by the orange glow of the burning cabin.

"I'm your father," he said. "*You wouldn't.*"

"Have you met you?" I asked, curling my lip. "I'm half you, remember?"

"You're half her, too."

His words sliced through me. He was right, but he was also trying to hit me where it hurt. I couldn't let him manipulate me, not now.

"Shoot now, and you'll be just like me," he said. "You liked that gun. You said it was pretty. Do you know what I use it for?"

"*Shut up,*" I snarled.

"I was saving it for King," he went on, his lip curling. "I was going to kill him for you."

"Liar!" I exclaimed. "You were going to hand me over. You were going to wire me up as a magical bomb and let them drain my blood. *Admit it.*"

"That's what I wanted them to think."

"*Don't.*"

"Do you think you're better off with Chaser and Gasket?" He took a step forwards. "They can't keep you safe from King, but I can."

"I don't believe you." I took a step back. "They killed my mum because of you."

Marini's expression hardened.

"Did you ever love her?" A tear slid from my eye as the revolver shook in my hands.

He stared at me and said nothing.

"Answer me!"

"Once," he said, devoid of emotion. I drew in a shaky breath as he took another step towards me. "But she was stupid, just like you are now. Getting into bed with Chaser, planning a coup with Gasket, murdering Rick. Look at what you've brought down on the pack. You're not better than me...*you are me*. You are my daughter. You are a Marini, Betty, but like you said yourself. *You're half her*. Half murderer, half *stupid*. You're damaged goods, little girl. That's why you'll never be able to pull that trigger."

My breathing quickened and rage boiled through my veins. He never loved me. He never cared. There was nothing inside him but greed, hate, and depravity.

"You're right," I said, tossing the gun, which clattered to the ground. "I can't pull the trigger."

Marini smirked. "Come with me and we'll take down the Hollow Men together. Come with me, Betty, and I'll show you what it's like to be a Marini."

"It's like I said," I began, feeling the power of the moon come to life inside me, "I'm half you, *Dad*."

My body erupted in an inferno of pain as I turned, my limbs twisting and reshaping faster than I thought possible. My clothes ripped and fell away, fur sprouted, teeth elongated, and I lunged.

I collided with a stunned Marini, knocking him flat on his back. My paws held him down and I snapped my jaws at his throat, the wolf taking control of the hunt.

Warmth burst into my mouth as I tore flesh, ripping apart the werewolf beneath me. The one-time alpha of the Fortitude Wolves shredded like soggy paper until his struggle ceased.

Standing over him, I watched as his blood bloomed from his chest, staining his shirt, and leaking into the grit underneath him. His gaze met mine and he let go of his last breath, the sound passing through me like his ghost had rushed through my body on its way to Hell.

Lifting my head, I looked to the moon and howled.

The alpha was dead.

CHAPTER 27

CHASER

"**S**loane!"

I watched her sprint into the bush after Marini and sprang into action. I'd barely taken a step when a hand grasped my ankle. Looking down, I saw Rocket clawing at me, blood seeping from between his lips.

"*Bastard*," he rasped. "I'll kill you, you piece of shit."

"*Get the hell off me.*" I aimed my gun, but he knocked my knee out from underneath me, and I stumbled.

The shot went wide, ricocheting off the hard ground and disappearing into the darkness.

Rocket lunged and knocked me to the ground. We fell in a heap, the force dislodging my grasp on my gun, and it skidded across the packed dirt of the clearing, but I didn't need it. His movements were sluggish as we struggled, and it didn't take me long to get him on his back.

He was weak—the gunshot must've clipped an artery. Soon the blood loss would cause him to lose consciousness, and it would all be over. This was a last-ditch attempt to get another blow in before he bit the dust.

"Coward," Rocket exclaimed, thrashing beneath me. "You were never Fortitude."

"Of course not," I said, curling my hands around his neck. "I was bound by magic, arsehole." I squeezed, my face contorting as his eyes bulged.

He deserves it, I thought. *He deserves what he's getting and then some.*

"Chaser!"

I glanced up at Gasket, who'd appeared out of the smoke, and Rocket coughed beneath me. *Just kill him*, a voice in the back of my mind said. *Just end it already.*

"We need him alive," the wolf commanded.

I felt the will of the talisman bear down on me and with a roar of frustration, I smashed my fist into Rocket's temple and he went slack. With any luck, blood loss would get him before he woke up.

Gasket eyed him before grabbing me. "We need you around the side," he said. "We've got the rest of them boxed in."

I wiped the sweat off my forehead with the back of my arm. "How many?"

"Hard to say, but we've got more."

"Where's Sloane?" He glanced around, his forehead creasing. "Where is she?"

I narrowed my eyes and nodded towards the bush. "Marini got out."

"What?" He took a step towards the darkness, but it was my turn to hold him back.

"I want to go after her, too, but we're stuck here. She knows what she's doing."

"Are you sure about that? It's her father out there."

My lip curled. "If you're implying she'll hesitate, I'd think again."

He snarled before pushing me off him. "We need to end this. *Now*."

He didn't have to tell me twice.

I picked up my gun and followed the old wolf around the corner of the cottage, ducking behind the row of cars and joining the others.

I counted over our remaining men, knowing Hopper and DeLuca were out defending the women in the desert. We were down a few, but I knelt beside Spike, Watts, Stewie, Bones, Ram, and Ratchet. Behind another car were more faces I didn't know but were on our side of the divide.

"Rhodes?" I asked.

"He was shot," Spike said. "Butcher's got him."

I nodded as Gasket peered around the end of the car.

"It doesn't have to be this way," he called out over

the expanse. "Throw down your weapons, and this can all end right now."

A voice echoed from behind their barricade. "Eat shit!"

I raised an eyebrow. "That was creative."

"Fortitude as you knew it is over," Gasket went on, ignoring my sarcasm. "We can't go back now. Only forwards. Marini was leading the pack on a path to destruction, and you know it. Is that how you want to live your lives? Murdering for sport? That was never the Fortitude way."

"EAT. *SHIT*."

"I think they like the taste of shit," I said, leaning against the car.

"Courage in adversity," Spike said with a sigh.

"They've lost a lot of wolves," Ratchet noted. "There's gotta be only a dozen of them left."

"You want to shoot it out?" Ram asked. "We're running out of bullets."

"So are they."

"Wait." Spike slammed his fist against my shoulder, forcing my attention to shift from the standoff behind me to the darkness in front. "You hear that?"

In the distance, a howl echoed on the wind and the entire clearing seemed to fall into an eerie silence—even the renegades froze.

We stared at the shadows, every one of us tense, waiting to see what would emerge from the darkness.

Finally, a wolf slunk out of the tree line, its jaws

coated in blood. Her coat was almost black, with patches of chestnut, her eyes shining a rich copper. She was sleek, beautiful, and terrifying all at once.

Sloane.

Thumping Gasket on the chest, I went to meet her, my panic flaring as I ducked low in case the renegades opened fire. It was an emotion I hadn't felt for a very long time, and it unsettled me to my core. Was she hurt? Did Marini...

"Sloane?" I stood before her, but she didn't shift.

She stared up at me, her eyes sharp and calculating.

"You know what to do," I murmured, standing aside.

She padded across the clearing, passing the wolves who'd pledged their allegiance to Gasket, and into the open. All eyes were on her, all of them stunned, and some trembling.

She stood in the light of the burning cottage, the wind buffeting her fur, and even I felt the power of her presence. Everyone here couldn't deny who she was anymore.

The wolf who could turn at will. The wolf who had control over the moon itself.

She'd killed Marini, his blood was all over her, but it was the bond of the alpha that forced them to see.

The renegades murmured amongst one another, their voices rising. Some threw down their guns and fell to their knees, while others backed away. They made their choices and one by one, they moved.

Some wolves submitted and others fled. It was that simple.

Engines roared into life and I raised my head, the light from multiple headlights blinking across the clearing.

"They're on the run!" someone shouted, breaking the spell.

"We can't let them go," Watts said.

Sloane took a step towards me, her body quivering, then she turned.

It was over in a second, her limbs elongating and snapping, her fur shedding, until she stood in front of the pack naked, smeared with dirt and blood. She blinked, dazed by the light, then collapsed.

I rushed forwards and caught her in my arms before she hit the ground.

Gasket slid to his knees beside us and pressed his palm to Sloane's forehead. "She's burning up."

"She..." I was having trouble reconciling that she'd torn apart her own father, and by the looks of it, so was she.

"Go," Gasket said. "Get her out of here."

I glanced at the retreating wolves.

"They're not your problem," Gasket said. "Sloane can't stay here. They know the truth and will use it against us. Against *her*." He pressed the talisman into my hand. "Protect her, Chaser."

I nodded as he rose to his feet and strode across the yard, silhouetted by the fire. He lifted his fingers to his lips and whistled, the sound slicing through the air. "Everyone with me!"

As the roar of revving engines filled the clearing, I scooped Sloane into my arms and carried her to the nearest car. The convoy tore out of the yard and onto the road, pursuing the remaining renegades towards the highway as I bundled her into the passenger seat.

Fastening the seat belt, I paused, combing her bloodied hair away from her face with my fingers.

The things she'd been forced to do... Her transformation... No wonder she'd collapsed. She wasn't made for this. Killing her own father. No one should have to do that. No one at all.

"It'll be okay," I murmured. "I'll get you out of here."

CHAPTER 28
SLOANE

I was vaguely aware I was dreaming.

Cool air was blowing on my skin, making a strand of my dark hair flutter back and forth in the breeze. The tickling sensation on my neck roused me further, though I fought it with all I had. Waking wasn't something I wanted to do right now. Out there, beyond my closed eyelids, was reality. And reality sucked.

Despite my struggle, my eyes cracked open and I swatted at the stray hair, tucking it behind my ear. Raising my head, I glanced around the unfamiliar room. Was I dreaming? This place looked a hell of a lot like one of those nondescript motel rooms Chaser and I had stayed in during our road trip.

The ceiling was slathered in that awful popcorn plaster I'd become so familiar with, and the closed curtains had a putrid floral pattern. The laminate floor was bubbling where it met the white walls, and there was a mildew stink that seemed to cling to everything —even the scratchy sheets on the bed were rank with it.

Hell, this was one of those awful '...and then she woke up and found out it was all a dream' plot devices movies used. I didn't want to one-star review my life, but it was better than acknowledging the last two months were real.

I pushed up, my head feeling like it was stuffed with cotton wool. Picking at my hair, I sniffed it. Smoke...and blood. I wet my lips. They tasted like blood, too.

"Chaser?"

Movement from across the room startled me. A chair scraped back, and he was there.

"Sloane." He sat beside me, his hand combing through my tangled hair.

"It wasn't a dream, was it?" I whispered, my eyes gritty and dry.

He shook his head. "No. It was very real."

"Where are we? For a moment, I thought..."

"We're at a motel near the New South Wales border."

I jerked away from his touch and scooped the musty sheets around me. "But..."

"We weren't followed," Chaser said, his forehead creasing. "No one knows we're here."

"You're doing it again," I exclaimed. "You're—"

"Shh," he murmured. "Listen to me. I won't let anything happen to you, you hear?"

He reached for me, and I let him pull me into his arms. Nestling into his neck, I clutched onto his T-shirt, feeling the hard plane of his chest. His heart was thrumming wildly underneath my palm. *Ba-boom, ba-boom...*

"I killed him, Chaser," I murmured. "I..."

"I know." His hand soothed over my back.

One half of our revenge plan had come to fruition —albeit, not as planned—but at what cost? Had I shaved a piece of my soul off the moment I tore out Marini's throat? He was a monster, but he was my father. *He was my father.*

"What happened?" I asked with a shake of my head.

"The renegades retreated," Chaser explained, giving me a rundown. "We had the upper hand, but when you came out of the bush as a wolf... Some bowed to you, and some ran. Gasket and the others went after them, and I brought you here."

"The talisman?"

"I have it."

I breathed deeply and pressed my hands over my face. "Good, I..." I hesitated. I'd expected more bloodstains, but my skin was clean. "Did you...?"

"Bathe you?" He smirked and ran his hand through my hair. "Sure did."

"*Pervert.*"

He chuckled, his smile changing his entire face. It was so startling, I hesitated, the thought triggering something else inside me. I'd changed, too.

"What?" he asked.

"Because I... Does that mean...? Am I alpha now?"

"Technically, but they'll follow Gasket until you're ready."

I tensed. After everything that'd happened, I knew I wasn't cut out for it. The bravado I'd had when I'd arrived at the compound was foolish and arrogant. I was the wrong choice if all it took was my abnormal abilities.

"It's his now," I whispered. "I want him to have it."

"Are you sure?"

"Yes, one hundred percent. Maybe one day, but not now. The pack will be reborn under Gasket for the better."

Chaser nodded. "Yes, it will."

Liberated from Marini's psychotic rule, those who were left would flourish with Gasket at the helm. It would take a long time to build the pack back up, but maybe they'd become something better than they'd been. A true family.

"What if they don't find the renegades?" I asked. "They'll come back for us, won't they?"

"They'll always have it out for you," Chaser replied. "You, me, Gasket, and the others."

"Good. If they come calling, I'll be ready for them."

"You and me both."

Lifting my head, I rubbed my eyes, uneasiness making my stomach roll with nausea. "So what now?"

"We rest, regroup, and plan," he replied. "Nothing has to happen today."

"The Hollow Men..."

"Sloane..." Chaser sighed and lowered his gaze as if he were suddenly shy.

"Don't do that." Cupping his cheek, I gently lifted his chin. "You being vulnerable is too weird to handle."

He snorted, his lips quirking. "What have you done to me?"

"I didn't do anything," I whispered, my heart swelling. "It was the stars, remember?"

His lips met mine, and my arms snaked around his neck. Warmth spread through me as his tongue swept over mine, his touch electrifying my skin everywhere his fingers went. Up and down my spine, along the curve of my neck, sparking on my cheek. Finally, he pulled back, lingering as if he didn't want to be parted from me.

"Do you realise we don't have to pretend anymore?" I asked, my lips brushing against his.

"Yeah." His admission was a sigh so heavy, it rooted itself in my soul.

It'd taken a long time to get here, but now... We had one last hurdle before forever. *The Hollow Men.*

He and I both knew it without having to utter the words. We'd talked about it at the compound and out in the bush under the stars where Chaser had shown me part of his soul. We'd talked about our future, but neither of us saw one unless our last enemy was put down and our demons were laid to rest.

Chaser and I couldn't love until both our pasts were buried. And he couldn't truly be free until he was released from the magic binding him to the talisman.

I combed my hands through his messy hair, not afraid of my feelings for him anymore. "We have today...then tomorrow, we begin."

"Tomorrow," Chaser echoed.

Tomorrow...

OTHER BOOKS IN

THE FORTITUDE WOLVES TRILOGY...

Werewolves and vampires are embroiled in a war for supremacy and a troubled woman is in the centre of it all...only she doesn't know it.

Packed with suspense, action, and supernatural secrets, this series is sure to keep readers on the edge of their seats...

Wolf Called #1

Wolf Fated #2

Wolf Hunted #3

WOLF HUNTED

(Fortitude Wolves - Book Three)

A werewolf civil war. A vampire blood ritual. To stop both, werewolf Sloane will have to go to war.

Barely escaping with their lives, Sloane and Chaser are on the run.

The Fortitude Wolves are split down the middle, the Hollow Men are on their tail, and the threat of death hangs over their head at every turn. Their only choice is to keep their heads down and find a way to end the madness once and for all.

Short on friends, Sloane is backed into a corner with little hope remaining. Her only way out is through a maniacal vampire who wants to sacrifice her in a blood ritual—which isn't her idea of a happy ever after.

But in the darkness of the Australian bush, an unexpected visitor may have the answer she's been searching for. An answer to a question she never dreamed of asking.

If they want their forever, Sloane and Chaser must make their final stand and go for broke...*or die trying.*

Wolf Hunted is the final book in the Fortitude Wolves trilogy. Werewolves and vampires fight for ultimate power

*in this thrilling conclusion to this suspenseful Urban
Fantasy series.
Will Sloane and Chaser make it out alive?
Their only choice, is all out war.*

ABOUT NICOLE

Nicole R. Taylor is an Australian Urban Fantasy author.

She lives in the western suburbs of Melbourne dreaming up nail biting stories featuring sassy witches, duplicitous vampires, hunky shapeshifters, and devious monsters.

She likes chocolate, cat memes, and video games.

When she's not writing, she likes to think of what she's writing next.

Follow Nicole Online:

Website: nicolertaylorwrites.com
Facebook: facebook.com/nrtaylorwrites
Newsletter: nicolertaylorwrites.com/newsletter

www.ingramcontent.com/pod-product-compliance
Lightning Source LLC
Chambersburg PA
CBHW060814190726
48285CB00002B/666